Mason

Striking Back: Book Two

S.M. SHADE

Copyright © 2015 S.M. Shade

Cover Art by Kellie Dennis at Book Cover by Design: www.bookcoverbydesign.co.uk

Interior Formatting by That Formatting Lady: www.facebook.com/ThatFormattingLady/

All rights reserved. No part of this publication may be reproduced, distributed, or transmitted in any form or by any means, including photocopying, recording, or other electronic or mechanical methods, without the prior written permission of the publisher, except in the case of brief quotations embodied in critical reviews and certain other noncommercial uses permitted by copyright law.

This is a work of fiction. Names, characters, businesses, places, events and incidents are either the products of the author's imagination or used in a fictitious manner. Any resemblance to actual persons, living or dead, or actual events is purely coincidental.

Table of Contents

Prologue 1
Chapter One 3
Chapter Two 14
Chapter Three 22
Chapter Four 29
Chapter Five 40
Chapter Six 49
Chapter Seven 58
Chapter Eight 65
Chapter Nine 70
Chapter Ten 79
Chapter Eleven 91
Chapter Twelve 96
Chapter Thirteen 109
Chapter Fourteen 123
Epilogue 133
Acknowledgments 134
More from S.M. 136

Prologue

Everly

Something is wrong. Really wrong. I can't remember what it is. Danny tried to drown me, and I almost died. If Mason hadn't shown up…

Mason! My eyes fly open as my horrific discovery floods back. Mason is a monster, a sex slave trafficker, and he had me kidnapped.

My heart tries to escape my chest as I gaze frantically around the room. I'm tucked in Mason's bed, wearing nothing but an oversize t-shirt and panties. I suppose I should be grateful I'm not in a dungeon. Yet. The thought gets me moving, albeit slowly. Whatever the asshole drugged me with is still dragging me down. I'm shocked to see it's almost noon. I must've been out for over twelve hours.

Biology overcomes fear for the moment and I creep into the adjoining bathroom to relieve myself. I'm so thirsty, it feels like my tongue is glued to the roof of my mouth. Hoping no one will hear, I turn the sink on and gulp water from the faucet.

My footsteps to the bedroom door are careful, soft. I can't hear anything, the house is silent. Is he gone? Am I locked in? Finding my jeans and shoes by the chair, I dress quickly, trying to force my fuzzy brain to think. My first instinct is to try to escape through the window since we're on the first floor. No doubt that will set off his security alarm though, and right now I'm barely strong enough to stay on my feet. I'd never outrun him or his goon.

A phone. I need to get to a phone and call Ian. He knows where Mason lives and can send the police. Damned if I can remember the address. I'm surprised when the door handle turns easily, and I expect to see someone guarding the door, but the hallway is empty.

So is the living room. No phone in sight, though. Shit. What do I do? Do I chance searching the house to call for help, or try to escape? The front door is right there, tempting me. It's afternoon, surely there will be people around. Someone. Anyone. Screw it. I have to get out of here. My hand lights on the doorknob for a split second when I'm frozen by his voice.

"Are we going to do this again, Everly?"

Chapter One

Mason

A stray puppy wandered into my yard last year, skinny and starving. It managed the energy to run when I approached it, and found itself cornered by my back fence. I'd never seen such wide, terrified eyes. Until now.

What the fuck? Why is she so afraid of me? I know finding the fake documents and ID's confused her, but I don't know why it caused her to panic. Does she think I'd hurt her? Part of me wants to let her go. Call Ian to come get her, but I can't let her leave until I know where her head is.

My security guard, Devon, drugged her to get her back here. I can't have her running to the cops with stories of fake ID's and kidnapping. Everything I've worked so hard to build will disintegrate, and I can't risk it. First, I have to make her understand. I have to do something to take that look of terror from her face. It's tearing me up.

"Please," she whispers. "Just let me go. Don't do this." She flattens her back against the door as I approach her, and tears fill her eyes when I take her trembling hand. Her whole body is shaking, and she keeps blinking like she's trying to focus her eyes. I know she doesn't have much tolerance for drugs. It's probably making her dizzy.

"You need to sit down before you fall."

"What the hell did you do to me?" she demands.

"It was a sedative. I'm sorry, but you jumped from a moving car. You were going to hurt yourself."

Her face hardens and anger shines in her eyes. "Guess you can't damage the merchandise. Let me go, and I won't say anything to anyone."

What the hell is she talking about? "Not until we have a chance to talk. Tell me why you ran."

Her hand tightens on the door knob. "You know why. I found your stash of ID's."

"So instead of asking me to explain, you run like a crazy person?"

"I also heard you on the phone. Girls, fake passports, thousands of dollars. You think I don't recognize a trafficking operation?"

"Trafficking?" After a moment of confusion, I'm struck by her accusation. Not just struck. Bashed. Pummeled. A physical pain twists my gut. She couldn't have hurt me worse if she'd stomped on my nuts. I love her, and she thinks I traffic in sex slaves. Doesn't bode well for our relationship, I have to admit.

"Evie…Christ…how could you think…?" It takes a moment for me to clear my head. Her fear is suddenly clear. Not only does she think I sell women, she assumes I'll do the same to her for finding out. "Sit down, Everly," I demand, trying to swallow my anger and devastation at her conclusion. "After I explain how fucking wrong you are, and what's really going on, I'll take you home. Or you can call Ian…or a cab…whatever."

"Just let me leave now and I'll never say anything."

"So help me, if you don't plant your ass on that couch, I will. Now." My tone brokers no argument, and she moves to the far end of the couch, her wary, fearful gaze tearing another strip from my soul.

"The passports and ID's are fake. You're absolutely right about that." I sit across from her, dragging my hands through my hair in frustration. I'm risking everything by sharing what I'm about to tell her. "You know I own multiple domestic violence shelters. You've seen what they do. How could you think I'd exploit women in such a horrible way?"

"I imagine it's a good cover. An endless supply of vulnerable prey."

Fuck, she's pissing me off. "The passports and ID's are for the women who escape husbands and boyfriends who are particularly dangerous." My gaze meets hers. "I'm going to tell you something that very few people know. I have to believe you'll keep it secret, no matter how little you think of me.

"I'm a part of an underground system, put in place for battered women and children. Sometimes, to keep them safe, we have to work outside the law. Many of them were married to cops, FBI agents, government officials, judges. People with reach, who aren't easy to escape."

Doubt begins to replace the fear on her face. "You get them fake ID's so they can leave the country?"

"It's more than that. We set them up with new lives, sometimes in other countries, but more often a new state. There's a network of people and privately owned charities who help them hide and start over."

Teeth clamp down on her lip, chewing as she thinks it over. "And the money?"

"We give them twenty-five thousand each to help with housing, food and expenses."

She wants to believe me, but I can tell she's struggling. "And you had to send your goon to chase and drug me to tell me this?"

"Evie," I sigh. "What would've happened if you'd gone to the cops, if they'd found the passports? Not only could it have shut down the whole operation, it would've left all those women and their kids exposed, vulnerable. They could've been found."

She cradles her head in her hands. "I can't think. I need some time. My head is killing me."

"It's a lot to comprehend with a sedative hangover. Will you stay put if I get you a drink?"

"Yes, thank you." I hate the way she sounds, the distance in her voice. She can be trusted, once I convince her I'm telling the truth. Given enough time, I would've explained everything to her anyway. But our relationship is over. There's a big difference between not trusting me, and thinking me capable of sex slavery.

She drains the glass of water after swallowing the ibuprofen I give her. "Do you remember Ivy Stevens?" I ask.

Her tired eyes regard me. "Of course. She lived at Striking Back a few months ago. She went back to her husband."

"That's the story we tell, but it isn't true." I sit beside her and log into Skype.

Ivy answers, smiling when she sees my face. "Mason! How are you?"

"I'm doing good. Someone wants to say hi." I hand my phone to Evie, who takes it cautiously.

"Hi, Ivy," she says.

"Hi Everly! It's Maia now. It's good to see you. Are you still working at Striking Back?"

"Of course. How are things?"

"Fantastic. I love it here. I have a new job, new friends. Everything's great. I'm glad to see you've joined the little secret society." She laughs.

"I'm just learning about it, actually," Evie replies softly.

I take the phone back and let Ivy know we'll check in again soon.

Everly stares at her feet, shaking her head. "I can't believe this was going on around me and I had no idea."

"I need to know you won't tell anyone, Evie. A lot of lives depend on it."

"I understand." Her soft brown eyes peek up at me through her lashes. "I'm sorry I got the wrong idea. I panicked."

"I'd never hurt you."

"I know."

I hand over her cell phone. "Call Ian. He called for you, earlier, and I told him you were sleeping." I retreat to my bedroom for a moment while she makes her call. I don't want her to leave, but I know this can't work. Christ, she thought I was going to sell her. How do I forget that? I can understand someone who doesn't know me jumping to such a conclusion if they heard and saw the things she did. But not her. It tears at something deep inside of me. I have to let her go.

She's still sitting on the end of the couch when I return. "He'll be here in a few minutes."

"Okay, you should rest until he gets here. You look pale."

Nodding, she curls up on her side, pulling a throw pillow under head. "I'm sorry, Mason."

"Me too, Evie."

Ian rings the bell, and Everly doesn't move a muscle. I let him in and lead him past her sleeping form to the kitchen. "I need to talk to you for a moment."

"Sure, what's going on? Ev sounded really upset. You guys fighting?"

"Not exactly. I'm taking a huge fucking chance with what I'm about to tell you, but I know Evie will need to talk to someone about it." He never blinks when I tell him about the underground shelters I'm a part of, and actually seems impressed.

"I can't believe Evie would have a problem with this, man. I mean, she's not exactly a law breaker, but she should understand why it's necessary."

"She doesn't have a problem with what I do." I explain what happened with the passports and the overheard phone call.

When I tell him the conclusion Evie jumped to, he shakes his head. "She thought you were selling women?"

"She freaked out and ran. I had to call one of my security guys to help me find her. She was hiding in the neighborhood, and I couldn't let her go to the cops. It would've destroyed everything. I just wanted to bring her back, explain what was really going on, but she fought him so hard. Even jumped from the car as he was bringing her back."

Ian looks devastated. "She must've been terrified."

"She was, but I didn't know why. Devon had to sedate her to get her back without hurting her. That's why she's so tired. I told her to call you. I just want her to feel safe, and I know she trusts you. Please keep an eye on her."

Ian blinks in surprise. "Are you breaking up?"

"After what she thought I would do to her? She doesn't trust me, and I don't think she ever will. She believed I'd sell her, abuse her."

"There's a reason behind that. It's not my story to recount, but Ev has had more than one experience with sexual assault at the hands of someone she trusted. I'm not saying it lead her to that conclusion, but I'm sure it helped."

I nod. It still doesn't change anything. "Danny is locked up so she should be okay to go home. I'm going to keep security on her for a while just in case. Just, please let me know if anything happens…if she needs anything. I know she won't tell me."

Ian gives a reluctant smile. "Evie acts tough, but underneath, she's a scared kid still waiting for the worst. She's never had anyone take care of her without some obscene ulterior motive before, so it's hard for her to accept."

We both glance toward the living room when we hear Everly call, "Mason?"

"Go on. Take her home. I'll be in touch when I find out Danny's court date. She'll have to appear." Ian nods, and I hear the front door close a few minutes later as he leaves with the only woman I've ever loved.

"Get up fuckwad!" Parker's shout sets off brass bells in my skull. My mouth tastes like the ass end of a coyote, and the feel of the hardwood floor digging in my ribs tells me I didn't make it to bed. Groaning, I pull myself up and onto the couch.

"You look like shit, brother," Alex says, shaking his head and sitting beside me.

"I had a late night. What do you two want?"

"A late night?" Parker scoffs. "You've been MIA for two

days. I know your girl thinks you're a human trafficker, but that's no reason to drink an entire liquor store."

"Fuck off, Park."

Alex hands me a cup of coffee, and Parker tosses a brown paper bag beside me. "Eat. Nothing better for a hangover than greasy food." Parker brags about banging some new chick as we eat sausage biscuits, but I barely hear him. I never drink until I pass out. I hate being out of control.

But I couldn't get Evie out of my head, and drinking to quiet the sound of her voice seemed like a good option. Apparently, it only works until I wake up. "Is everything under control at work?" I ask, wiping my hands on a paper napkin.

"Work's fine," Alex replies. "Now, go shower and let's go to the gym. I feel like kicking you in the head."

Although I feel like hell, I really don't want to spend another day home alone. "Give me ten minutes." After a quick shower, ibuprofen, and a bottle of water, I feel almost human. "I'll meet you there," I call, as Parker and Alex hop into Parker's truck.

As I follow them to the gym, I wonder what Evie is doing today. Did she return to Building Tomorrow's Child after one of the counselors nearly killed her? I'm sure she did. If there's one thing I know about that girl, it's that she's stubborn as hell. She won't let one psycho keep her from helping those kids. I hope that also goes for Striking Back. The women and children love her, and I'd hate for her to stop coming because we're over. I need to call later and see if she's been there.

The gym doesn't open for a few hours so we have the place to ourselves. Alex grins at me. "You have half an hour to warm up old man, then I'm coming for you."

"Look who's throwing his diaper into the ring," I tease. Relief shows on his face as he smiles, and I know he was worried about me.

Alex has always been the one who worries, who feels things more strongly. When our mother was killed, and we were forced to move to London with our aunt and uncle, he struggled more than me or Parker.

Hell, they were only eight, and in one horrible bloody

night, our world completely changed. Aunt Linda and Uncle Logan were suddenly the guardians of three heartbroken, extremely angry boys. Parker and I got into a few scuffles at school, but Alex made a damn habit of blacking eyes and busting lips.

After his second school suspension, they signed him up for MMA classes, and it didn't take long for me and Parker to follow him. We learned to fight the same way we do everything…together. We got through it, and Alex got a handle on his anger. I know he still struggles from time to time, but he's also the most compassionate person I've ever known.

After lifting weights and running on the treadmill for a few minutes, I gear up and meet Alex on the floor. "I'm registered for the Children's Hospital Charity Tournament. So don't go easy. I need to be ready," he informs me.

"Is Parker competing too?"

"Nope, but Taylor is." A wide smile spreads across his face.

"Brandon? How did you talk him into that?"

"Believe it or not, he asked me." Fourteen year old Brandon Taylor came to us almost a year ago. Skinny, shy, and afraid of his own shadow, he was being bullied at school and wanted to learn to fight back. After nearly a year of training, his self-confidence has soared along with his fighting skill. It doesn't hurt that he's grown six inches and packed on some muscle as well.

"You tell him I'll be there to watch," I say, throwing a front kick.

Alex easily knocks it down, bouncing around as we get warmed up. "The only spectator he gives a shit about is Karen."

"Ha! Good for him." The boy has good taste. Karen Michaels is a fifteen year old girl in our intermediate class. "No wonder he asked to test for intermediate."

Alex laughs and replies, "Young love."

"Horny teenage boy," I snort, sneaking in a reverse punch to his stomach. "Watch those reverse punches. You let too many through."

"I'm just building up your confidence." He catches me with a quick side kick to the ribs. "How long are you going to wait?"

"For what?"

"To straighten things out with Everly."

"Just shut up and fight."

His laugh echoes across the gym as he dodges the next reverse punch. "Don't be a fucking idiot. That girl is crazy about you."

"Yeah, when she isn't waiting for me to chain her in a dungeon."

"A misunderstanding," he replies, with a wave of dismissal. "Call her before you fuck up a good thing."

I throw a couple of combinations to try to shut him up. He doesn't understand, and I can't say she broke my goddamn heart without sounding like a pussy. "Worry about your own sex life."

"Would you rather hear how I bent Cooper over the arm of the couch and fucked him until he begged for mercy?" He drops his guard, and I take advantage, getting him to the mat and into a leg lock. "Fuck," he swears, tapping out.

We spend another hour sparring and working on Alex's technique. When we flop onto the bench, Parker tosses us each a bottle of water and joins us. "You're not blocking his reverse punch."

"Yeah, thanks, Captain Obvious."

"Don't make me drag you back out there and whip your ass."

"See how he has to wait until I'm already exhausted to talk shit?" Alex asks me, and I shake my head at them. They could go on all day. "Tell this idiot to call Everly," he says to Parker.

"Alex." My voice holds a warning.

As usual, he ignores me. "Don't you think he should at least try to work it out?"

Parker glances at me, a serious expression on his face for a change. "Look, man. I'm not going to tell you how to handle some chick, but I do think Everly is…different. She's good for you. For once, a woman isn't tripping over her own tongue just to get to you. She doesn't seem to give a shit about your money. Hell, she fought you every step of the way." He laughs, and I try to keep the grin off my face when I think of tricking her into our first date.

"I don't know if it's love or lust or whatever, but you were happier with her. I'd think about it. That's all."

"If I promise to think about it, will you both shut the fuck up?" Alex's phone rings and after a quick glance, he sends it to voicemail.

"Dodging Cooper already?" Parker teases.

"No, wasn't Cooper."

"Got a new guy?"

"Of course not." Alex starts removing his footgear.

"So, who was it?"

"Since when is it any of your fucking business?"

"Since you're acting so shady."

"Alex," I interrupt. "Is everything okay?"

"It was Indiana State Prison," he admits reluctantly.

"Gene's been calling you?" I ask, my voice tight.

"A few times."

"Have you talked to him?" Parker demands.

I put a hand on Parker's chest. "If Alex wants to talk to him, that's his choice, Park."

"I haven't answered. He's left messages. He wants to see us." He looks up, his light brown eyes slightly hopeful.

"I don't give two fucks what the bastard wants," Parker spits, stalking off to the locker room.

I agree with him, but I don't want Alex to feel he's being ganged up on. "Alex, if you want to go talk to him, I'll understand. Don't worry about Parker."

He shakes his head and asks softly, "You don't want to see him, just once? You don't have anything to ask him?"

"Like what?"

"Like why!" I sit back as he leaps to his feet, pacing. "Or how the fuck could he? Why didn't he think of us? He was our father!"

I pull him back down beside me, cupping the back of his sweaty head in my palm like I used to when he was young and upset about something. "No. Because no answer he gives would satisfy me."

After a few seconds, he nods. "I get that."

"Just do me a favor and let me know if you decide to visit or talk with him, okay? Parker doesn't have to know, but I want to know you're all right."

"I don't know what to do, but when I decide, you'll know."

"Okay then. Let's go see if Parker's over his tantrum and grab some lunch."

Chapter Two

Everly

Ian rolls up his car windows when a shiver runs through me. "Ev, you okay?"

"Mmm Hmm." Nothing is okay. The last twenty-four hours is a jumbled mess in my head. Mason holding me in the lazy river. Danny shoving my head underwater. Laughing in the haunted house. Hiding behind an abandoned house, frozen in fear. Mason's smile when he said he loved me. His devastated expression when I accused him of hurting women.

"Mason told me everything, Ev. The underground network, your…misunderstanding."

"I can't talk about it right now, okay? Please."

His hand squeezes my knee. "All right. For the record though, I think Mason's a good guy."

"I know he is." He's far too good for me.

Ian escorts me home and flops onto my couch, grabbing the remote. "I appreciate you coming to get me, but you don't have to stay and babysit. Danny's locked up. I'm safe."

He gives me an exasperated glance when I sit beside him. "Uh-huh." A little smirk appears on his face as he continues to channel surf.

"I mean it. I'm fine. You can go."

Sighing, he presses mute and tosses the remote on the

couch. "Ev, you're sluggish from the sedative and covered in road rash from jumping from a moving car. You don't think we have some things to talk about? You could've killed yourself. What the hell were you thinking?"

Shame sweeps through me, flooding my cheeks with color. "I couldn't do it again. Just be another…worthless hole for strangers to fill. I heard him talking about money for girls and all I could see was Frankie, smiling, telling me to behave so he could love me."

His expression softens and he takes my hand. "You were never worthless. You know that. None of it was your fault."

"I know."

"You freaked out."

"I guess so."

"You accused the guy of sex trafficking, Pup."

"I know. I fucked everything up," I moan, resting my forehead on my palm. "I was so scared to let that guy get me in Mason's car. I'd have done anything to escape."

"Obviously," Ian murmurs, putting his arm around me. "I don't blame you for being afraid. Frankly, the fact he drugged you really pisses me off. You weigh, what? One twenty soaking wet? He could've controlled you."

"He was protecting the women he rescues. I don't blame him. God, if I'd have brought the cops to his door, I'd have fucked up so many lives."

"But that didn't happen. Everyone is fine."

"I'm so sorry."

"Did you tell Mason that?"

I slump back on the couch, the weight of my guilt pulling me down. "Of course, but I don't think 'I'm sorry' is enough after accusing him of something so horrible. His face when he realized what I meant…shit, he was devastated."

"I'd imagine. You broke his heart. Look, Ev, I don't know fuck all about relationships, but I know when a guy has lost the fight. He loves you. It's all over his face when he says your name. He's a goner."

"It doesn't matter now. He'll never forgive me, and I don't

blame him."

Ian sighs and brushes my hair out of my eyes. "You don't know that. You need to talk to him. You're right, sorry isn't enough. You need to explain why you reacted that way. I know you hate to talk about it."

"No one knows but you," I whisper.

"You've never talked about it with anyone? None of the therapists or counselors they made us see at the home?"

I shake my head, and Ian pulls me into his embrace. "It's time, honey. If you love him, you need to let him in, let him know you so he understands your fears."

"I'll think about it. Right now, I'm exhausted. I just want to sleep. I still have to figure out what to do about BTC, whether to go back. I don't know."

"You don't have to have all the answers tonight. Get some rest."

Retreating to the bedroom, I toss and turn for nearly an hour, haunted by Mason's heartbroken expression before I finally fall asleep.

Ian has left for work when I wake up the next morning. My body feels heavy as I wander into the kitchen and grab a donut before plopping on the couch. Chunky ass be damned. Today, junk food is my friend.

I don't know what to do with myself. I'd usually be at Striking Back today, but there's no way I can go there now. I'm sure there's some rule that you don't visit a man's place of business after calling him a sex trafficker. While Striking Back was a big part of my days, and losing it will leave a hole in my life, it's nowhere near the crater that losing Mason has left.

It's only been twenty-four hours and I'm already miserable. His absence leaves me hollow and bleak, devoid of hope or purpose. Okay, maybe I'm being a little melodramatic. I was fine before I met Mason and life will go on without him. The man I love. People get dumped all the time, right? I mean, life's a bitch and love's another. I just need to keep busy so I won't think about him.

As if in response to my thoughts, Bill Carlin, the owner of

BTC, rings my phone. Shit. Is he going to ask me not to return? "Everly? How are you?" he asks after I accept the call. His voice is thick with concern.

"I'm fine. How is everything at BTC?"

He sighs. "Things are calming down. We've replaced Mr. Fennel with a new counselor, who the boys seem to like. I wanted to call to apologize for putting you in danger. I swear I ran background and criminal checks on that asshole, and they came back clean. If I'd thought for a minute he'd hurt you or anyone else…"

"You can't always predict psycho. It wasn't your fault."

"I just want you to know you'll be safe here. We'd hate to lose you."

"I love the kids and have no intention of leaving my volunteer position," I assure him. "Do you know what this afternoon's schedule is like?"

"It's park day. The whole group will be at Garfield Park if you'd like to join them."

"I'll be there, Mr. Carlin."

"I'm glad to hear it. If you have any issues at BTC, please let me know. I'll let the kids know you're coming."

"Thanks for calling," I reply, and disconnect the call. I force my stubborn body into the shower when all I want to do is crawl back under my covers and feel sorry for myself.

No matter how hard I try to keep him out, Mason invades my thoughts. As I wash, I close my eyes, recalling the feel of his strong hands lathering my hair when I was hurt. So gentle and caring. How could I have thought he'd hurt anyone? Once again, my issues have fucked up something good in my life.

My first day without Mason is long and tiring. I hit the gym, spend hours playing with the kids at the park, and go grocery shopping. Once I'm home, I clean my apartment, wash all my laundry, and rearrange my bookshelf. I've done my best to wear myself out, but to no avail. I still cry myself to sleep, staring at the empty space in the bed beside me.

The next few days are the same. I wake and struggle to find random ways to fill the hours until I can crawl into bed again. The gym. Book club. Drinks with Marie, BTC. Nothing feels right. Nothing can fill the Mason shaped hole in my life. Before him, I'd been alone for so long, ran from any kind of emotional relationship, that I'd forgotten how it felt to have someone. To love someone.

I hate this emotional shit. Why did I have to fall for him? And how much longer am I going to suffer because of it? Every day I want to call him and apologize, ask for another chance, but I can't make myself do it. After nearly a week, I'm shocked when Mason calls me.

My finger trembles as I press accept. "Hello?"

"Evie, it's Mason." His voice is hard, his words clipped.

"Uh…hey."

"Listen, I just got a call and your friend Macy has been taken to Community Hospital."

My heart leaps into my throat. "What happened? Is she okay?"

"I don't know the details. I'm on my way to find out now."

"So am I," I reply frantically, pulling on my shoes.

"She'll be okay. You be careful driving, you hear me?"

The concern in his voice sends an equal amount of hope and shame through me. Even after what I've done, he still cares. "I will. Mason…" I hesitate, bursting with so much I want to say, but this just isn't the time. "Thanks for calling."

"You're welcome. I'm just pulling in the lot. I've got to go. Drive safe." The call disconnects just as I jump into my Mini. I promised Macy I'd keep in touch after I dropped her at Striking Back, but I let my own shit get in the way of checking on my friend. Thank goodness I'm only a few minutes away from the hospital.

I spot Parker leaning against the wall outside Macy's room.

His eyebrows jump up when he sees me. "Everly! Hey, I guess you heard."

"Mason called me. Is she okay?" His hand wraps around my arm when I try to enter the room.

"She'll be okay. You can't go in right now. Cops are in there taking her statement."

"Cops? What the hell happened?"

Parker's eyes darken and narrow. "Her dickwad ex-boyfriend happened. She insisted on going back to work, since he hadn't bothered her in weeks. We had security escort her to her office door, but Al was waiting inside, hiding in the goddamn bathroom. He worked her over pretty good, Everly. It's not pretty."

Two officers leave the room, and Parker accompanies me inside. The sight of my usually vibrant friend looking so small and defenseless brings tears to my eyes. She has a large tube taped to her side and a cast covers her left ankle. Her face is a patchwork of bruises and puffy red skin. I hardly recognize her.

"Don't cry," she orders. "You'll get me started again."

"Oh, Mace, that son of a bitch. I'll kill him."

"Get in line, sweetheart," Parker growls.

"Do you want to tell me what happened?" I ask, sitting beside her and taking her hand.

"Jensen, the security guy, walked me to the door, and I told him I could take it from there. I mean, the damn door was locked...I never thought...anyway." She shakes her head and continues. "I hadn't been to work since I moved into Striking Back. I don't know how the hell he knew I'd come in today. The first couple of hours were fine, and it felt so good, Ev, to be back to normal, you know?" Her eyes fill with tears.

"It's okay."

"No, it isn't. I just wanted a piece of my life back, but the bastard has to take everything! He was hiding in the women's bathroom, and when I went in, he just started hitting me, screaming that I was a whore. My ankle snapped when he kicked it, and I fell to the floor. That's when he started kicking me in the face and chest. Janet, my assistant, must've heard something because she opened the door and saw him. She screamed for help, but by the time Jensen got to me, Al was gone."

"We'll get him," Parker says, his voice ice cold. "I swear to you. I'll find him."

Macy nods, wincing, and presses the button on her morphine pump. Her face relaxes and she looks up at Parker. "He'll show up here to finish the job while I can't run."

Parker sits carefully beside her on the bed and motions to the chair by the door. "That's my chair until you're discharged, honey. I'll be right there guarding this room until you go home. If I so much as take a piss break, your door will be locked. Get used to this pretty face because you'll be staring at it until this is over."

"Thank you," she slurs, the drugs taking over.

"Get some rest. You're safe with me."

Macy's eyes slam shut, and I wipe the tears from mine. As Parker moves from her bed toward the chair, I grab him in a firm hug. These brothers are too good to be true. "Thank you for watching over her."

Gently, he hugs me back. "It's what I do." When he releases me, I look up into the clear blue eyes I've been missing for a week. A mischievous smile crosses Parker's face as he spots his brother. "We're busted, baby," he says to me before turning to Mason. "Wasn't my fault, bro. She was all over me. She's relentless. Don't blame her, though. It's this new cologne…drives the women crazy."

Mason smirks and slaps him on the back of the head. His expression sobers when he regards me. "I talked to the doctor. She has a broken ankle, two broken ribs, and a punctured lung. She'll fully recover, but she'll be here at least a few days."

"I should get her some clothes, her stuff from S.B."

"Ms. Den is handling that." I hate the detachment I hear in his voice.

I nod, unsure what to say next as a nurse steps in and smiles at us. "She'll be sedated and sleep until morning. You may want to come back then." She turns to Parker before leaving the room. "I'll have a cot brought in for you."

Mason raises his eyebrows, and Parker laughs. "I told her

I'm the watch dog."

"I'll send Devon to relieve you tonight," Mason offers.

"No, I've got this."

"Suit yourself. I'll come by in the morning."

"I guess I'll go," I tell Parker. "Call if she asks for me, okay? My number's in her phone."

"Sure thing."

Nervously, I turn to Mason. "Can I talk to you? Just for a minute?"

His adam's apple jumps as he swallows. "Let's grab a coffee in the cafeteria."

It's early afternoon and the cafeteria is nearly empty as I slide into a booth across from Mason. He hasn't said a word since we left Macy's room. My hand shakes as I reach to take his. "I'm so sorry, Mason."

"You've said that, Evie. I know you are."

"I want to explain…why I thought…"

"I was a predator luring vulnerable women into a life of sexual slavery?" His hard tone doesn't conceal the pain in his voice.

My gaze falls to the table. "You have every right to be pissed at me, to hate me. I'm not trying to make excuses. I just want a chance to tell you why I jumped to such a horrible conclusion. There are things you don't know—nobody knows—but I can't talk about it here. Can you come by tonight? Just give me a few minutes and I won't bother you again."

Two rough fingers lift my chin until my eyes meet his. "I don't hate you, couldn't even if I tried, Evie."

I nod, and he sighs, shaking his head like he thinks he's making a mistake. "Eight o'clock?"

"Huh?" I mutter, surprised by his acceptance.

"Is eight o'clock okay?"

"Oh, yeah, eight's good."

He gets to his feet and drops a chaste kiss on my cheek. "See you then."

Chapter Three

Mason

My head isn't where it should be. Damn Evie and her soft brown eyes. I've tried to get her out of my mind all week with no success. Then she turns those remorseful eyes on me, pleading for a chance to explain, and I can't say no.

My day has been shit already. A woman I swore to protect has been attacked. I should be focused on how to update our security protocols, not thinking about how Evie's lips felt around my cock. Fuck, I still want her and not just in bed. I miss talking with her, her quick wit and ability to throw my teasing right back at me. She's fun, adventurous, and so compassionate. Shit. I'm done in.

I've cared for women before, even thought I loved them, but it's nowhere near how this stubborn woman makes me feel. Every inch of me wants to give this relationship another chance, but I'm not sure I can. It's not that I can't forgive her. I just need to know every time something goes wrong or scares her, she won't run away.

My usual confidence is nowhere to be found when I knock on her door. I have no idea what I'm going to do. I'm met with an uncertain smile when she opens the door and I'm struck by the heartbreaking thought this may be the last time I see her smile.

Any other woman hoping to reconcile—if that's what she

wants—would be dressed up and wearing a ton of makeup. I can't help but grin as she stands before me in worn jean shorts and a tee shirt, her face clean and hair pulled back in a simple ponytail. It's just so Evie. This is who she is and I can take her or leave her. Damn, I want to take her.

We settle on the couch, and she looks like she'd rather be anywhere else in the world when she says, "I have trouble trusting people, believing they are who they appear to be."

"I kind of figured that out, sweetheart."

Her hands twist in her lap. "But I want you to know why…well…I don't really want you to, but I think you need to and…"

I grip her hands in mine, stilling them and her nervous babble. "It's okay. You can tell me anything. Just take your time."

Resigned, she leans against the back of the couch and begins. "I told you I was five when my parents died and I was put into the foster care system. The first few places I was sent were terrible. Too many kids shoved into tiny rooms full of bunk beds. Little supervision. The older kids tortured me, stole my food.

"I didn't speak for nearly a year and finally the school alerted social services. I was taken in by a married couple, Frankie and Jeanette. It was like paradise compared to where I'd been. I had my own room and there were no other kids. They fed me, took me to the doctor…took care of me. I went to therapy twice a week and eventually started talking again. I was happy. For a while."

She swallows and gets to her feet. "I need a drink. Do you want some wine?"

"Sure, sounds good." I know she's trying to get her thoughts straight, gather her courage for whatever she's going to reveal. Avoiding my eyes, she hands me a glass of wine and places hers on the coffee table.

"Jeanette was a lawyer so she worked long hours. Frankie traded stocks and worked from home. He was the one who met me every day after school, who helped me with my homework and tucked me in at night." Her voice wobbles and she takes another gulp of wine.

"I'd lived with them for almost a year and they were

talking about adopting me. I finally had a family again, a mom and dad. But shit like that just doesn't happen, does it?" she spits bitterly.

"Anyway." Her hair falls into her eyes as she shakes her head, and I reach slowly to tuck it behind her ear, earning me a small smile. "Frankie said he loved me, that I was the daughter he always wanted. And I wanted a father so bad, Mason," she moans, her eyes pleading with me to understand. "That I let him do what he wanted to me. Let him touch me, fuck me," she confesses.

"Fuck," I mutter. I was really hoping her story wasn't leading there.

"I know. It's disgusting." A tear slips from her eye and she scrubs it away.

"No, Panda, not you." I pull her into my lap and wrap my arms around her. "What he did was disgusting. Unforgivable."

"He taught me to swim, and to ride a bike. He went to school and chewed out the principal when I was getting bullied. He was always there, acting like a dad, like he loved me. So when he started touching me I told myself that was how dad's showed their love. That's what he used to say. Behave and let me show you I love you."

"How old were you?"

"It started when I was almost nine. For a year, he only touched me, made me touch him. Then Jeanette landed a big case and started staying overnight at her office more and more. He took advantage of her absence and started fucking me."

"Oh, love, I'm so sorry." Her face is buried in my neck as I ask, "Did he go to jail for raping you?"

"I don't think you can call it rape," she scoffs. "I told you. I let him. I didn't want to get sent back to a group home or somewhere worse…and I thought he loved me."

She gasps as I grip her jaw and force her to look at me. The shame and misery in her eyes tears a strip from my heart. "Listen to me, Everly. It was absolutely rape. He groomed you, gained your trust, and then abused you. If you heard this story from one of the kids at BTC, would you blame them?"

"Of course not!"

"If a grown man molested then slept with one of those girls, would it be rape?"

She gnaws her lip before replying, "Yes."

"But with you it wasn't?"

"I...shit...I don't know."

"Yes, you do. It wasn't your fault, baby. You know. You just have to accept it." Finally, I get a small nod. "How did it stop, sweetheart?"

"A few days after my tenth birthday, Frankie invited his friend Mark over for dinner. We played video games and ate pizza. It was fun...until bedtime. When Frankie came to my room, Mark was with him."

Oh fuck, no. I don't want to hear this.

"He said Mark had a little girl and he was going to join us to learn how to love her. I said no, begged him not to let Mark touch me. I fought and screamed, bit and scratched, but he held me down until Mark was finished."

Her chest jumps as her breath hitches. All I can do is hold her tighter. "They were rough, and it hurt so badly. That's what I remember most. The pain and the blood. They wouldn't stop coming at me, and I eventually passed out while they were still taking turns.

"When I woke, they were gone. Someone had changed my sheets and cleaned me up. If it weren't for the pain in my crotch and stomach, I would've thought I dreamed the whole thing."

"What did you do? Who did you finally tell?"

She climbs off my lap and draws up her legs, clasping her arms around her knees. "I didn't tell anyone. I ran away." Her tortured eyes meet mine. "It's what I do."

"Not from me, Evie. Not anymore."

She nods and continues, "The cops picked me up a day later and took me to the group home where I lived until I aged out."

"Everly." She leans into my hand as I stroke the side of her face. "I'm so fucking sorry you went through that. If I find that guy, he's a dead man."

Her soft hand slides into mine. "It's long past. I'm sorry I let it fuck up what we had. I just...if a man could spend a year convincing me he loves me, making me love him, then let some stranger rape me..."

"Your new boyfriend being a sex trafficker isn't that much of a leap. I get it, baby."

"This is why I don't do relationships. I've got more issues than Time Magazine. It's not fair to you. I'm sorry."

Her expression tears me apart. Regret and guilt war with shame and pain. But there's something else there, a sliver of relief after finally sharing her nightmare, a glimmer of hope that I'll understand, that maybe it isn't too much. "You never told anyone?" I ask.

"Ian knows some of it. I don't want anyone to know, but I know I hurt you, and I want you to know that it wasn't about you. You were so good to me. I trust you never to tell anyone, even if we can't remain friends."

Christ, what am I going to do with her? "I can't be your friend, Everly."

Her gaze falls to the sofa cushion as she nods. "I understand."

"I don't fuck my friends and I sure as hell don't fall in love with them." The shock reflected on her face when I scoop her onto my lap almost makes me laugh. "You're mine, Evie. Mine to love and protect. The sooner you accept that, the better."

Warm arms wrap around my neck so tight I can hardly breathe. "I love you."

"I love you too, sweetheart." I take a second to inhale her scent, coconut mixed with something I can't place. So sweet. "Now, grab your stuff. You're coming back to my place tonight."

"Don't tell me what to do," she teases, poking me in the ribs. "Love won't keep me from kicking you in the balls."

"There's my stubborn spitfire." Her soft lips open in surprise when I take them in a passionate kiss. I missed this, missed her so much, her voice, her smell, her taste. I want to throw her in bed and show her what she's been missing, but it won't be tonight. After the conversation we just had, I'm sure sex is the last thing on her mind.

A soft moan rattles her throat as we break apart, and she

rests her forehead against mine. "I really can't tonight...my head's screwed up."

"No sex, love. I just want you with me."

"It's the only place I want to be," she murmurs, climbing off my lap.

"Of course, I expect you to feed me," I tease.

"To what?" she quips, flashing a quick grin.

"Do you always have to have the last word?"

"Of course not." She pulls on her shoes and heads to the bedroom.

"Good."

"Fantastic," she calls from her room.

Stubborn woman.

Everly chews her lip, looking uncertain as she crawls into bed with me. She's been understandably quiet tonight after revealing her past. "I just want to hold you, love, and wake up to that beautiful face in the morning."

Her body relaxes, molding perfectly to mine, and I rest my chin on her soft hair as she lays her head on my shoulder. "Will you still be able to look at me the same?" she asks softly. "You know...when we have sex? Would you rather I hadn't told you?"

Her eyes widen when I grip her chin, tilting her head until she has to look at me. "I see the same loving, compassionate, sexy as fuck woman I fell in love with. You aren't defined by the horrible things that happened to you. I'd do anything to go back and keep those bastards from hurting you, but your past has made you who you are. My Panda. And I wouldn't change you for one second."

Glazed eyes fill with relief, and she presses a soft kiss to my lips. "You're perfect, and I'm terrified I'm going to screw this up again," she confesses.

"I've made mistakes too, baby. We haven't known each

other very long, and we have a lot to learn. So no, I don't wish you hadn't told me. I want to know everything about you."

Soft fingers dance through my chest hair as she replies, "I didn't think I'd ever fall in love. It happened so fast. It scared the shit out of me."

Chuckling, I kiss her forehead. "Me too. Once you stood still long enough to let me love you. Just promise me, no matter what happens, you'll come to me, let me explain. No more running."

"I promise. What you do for those women is amazing, Mason. You're putting your own freedom at risk. Is that why your father is in prison? Did he start it, and you took over?"

I can't help the snort that escapes, and Evie sits up, gazing at me. I guess it's not fair to hide my shit after she so bravely shared hers.

"My father is a murderer. He's on death row."

Chapter Four

Evie

Holy shit. I stare down at Mason. "Are you serious?"

"No," he scoffs, "I only said it to impress you. Women love a guy with killer blood in his veins." Mason sits up, leaning back against the headboard.

"Do you want to tell me about it?"

"Like you said, Evie, I don't want to, but you need to know. I want you to understand why I could never hurt a woman, why I've done my best to protect them."

I take his hand, and he squeezes it. "My father killed my mother. He abused her for years and my brothers and me as well, to a lesser extent. She tried to shield us from him, from his temper, but as we got older he came after us more and more."

His face softens as he gazes into the distance. "She was beautiful, Evie, like you, and so damn brave. It was an average day when she picked us up at school and announced we weren't going home. She'd been saving what money she could for years, hiding it in her friend's account. She rented an apartment and a friend helped her move our stuff while we sat in school, clueless about how our lives were going to change.

"She found a job in a doctor's office as a receptionist. The move meant we'd have to change schools, but we didn't care. It meant moving into a worse neighborhood, and walking or taking a bus everywhere because we didn't have a car, but we were happy, the four of us."

"Were you hiding from your father?" I ask.

"No. He was pissed, but he thought she'd never make it on her own with three kids. He tried the penitent act at first. Apologizing, even buying a few things for us, clothes and stuff. Until she filed for divorce. At that point he knew she wasn't coming back. That's when he started stalking her."

"Did she involve the police?"

"Yeah, and you've seen how much help they are." I'm met with a stony expression when I look into his eyes. "She filed for a restraining order, citing physical abuse and stalking. They denied it on insufficient evidence. He was sitting in the living room when we got home from school, and the look on his face was terrifying. I knew I was seeing a man who just didn't give a fuck anymore.

"Mom shooed us from the room, but I snuck into the hall to listen. I also brought the twin's little recorder, hoping to catch his threats, show evidence to the judge. My father sat back on the couch, his ankle propped on his knee and said, 'I've had enough of this shit, Monica. You're going to call that piss ant lawyer and stop the divorce. You're bringing my boys home and that's final.'

"She faced him like she had a hundred times before. Her voice was steady as she replied, 'No, you're going to leave or I'm calling the cops. Quit calling my job and trying to get me fired. They know I have a psycho ex, so it won't work. They want to help, will even come to court if I ask and testify you're harassing me.' I'd never seen a man move so fast. He was on top of her, hitting her, and I couldn't just stand by anymore. I don't know what I thought I could do when he was four times my size, but at least I drew his attention from her."

Mason's voice is monotone, robotic. I don't think he even realizes I'm still there. It appears I'm not the only one unaccustomed to saying my story aloud. I want to grab him, hold him, but I want him to get it out, so I stay quiet and let him continue.

"His arm wrapped around my chest as he turned me toward my mother and said, 'I'll have them every other weekend, all alone. Hell, I might even win custody.' His hand slid around my throat, choking me, until Mom gave in and told him we'd come home. To just give her a couple days to get shit straightened out. She told him what he wanted to hear so he'd let me go."

"So you moved back home?" I ask, running my hand down his arm.

A small smile tilts his lips. "No. She called the cops the second he left. Her lawyer got an emergency hearing for a restraining order set for the next morning."

"She was brave," I remark, and he nods. "What happened at the hearing?"

I swear I can feel the heartbreak in his deep sigh. "The judge was a friend of my father's brother, who was the chief of police in Marion County. We never had a chance. The judge spent ten minutes chewing out my mom for trying to separate a father and his children, while she stood there with a black eye."

"Oh, fuck, Mason, no." I'm furious on his behalf. They must have felt so hopeless, watching the law take the abuser's side.

"I was glad my brothers weren't there. Mom made them go to school, but I'd threatened to walk to the courthouse if I had to." Dark hair flops in his eyes as he shakes his head, and I smooth it off his forehead. "He grinned at me. I remember that like it just happened. The way the bastard grinned at me, like he'd won the lottery, instead of the right to beat his wife.

"The lawyer gave us a ride back to the apartment, babbling about an appeal, but Mom didn't answer him. She looked so lost and afraid. I wanted to kill everyone involved for the tears that ran down her cheeks. The judge, the cops, the lawyers.

"She must've felt terribly alone," I murmur, swallowing the lump in my throat.

"She was alone. She sent the twins to stay at a friend's house that night, in case he showed up. She wanted me to go too, but I wouldn't leave her alone. She told me to hide and call 911 if he showed up, made me promise not to get between them or even let him see me.

"We spent the evening jumping at every little noise. When it got past midnight, we started to hope he wouldn't come. I tried to stay awake after she made me go to bed, but at some point, I fell asleep. My mother's scream woke me just before dawn. I heard her pleading with him, and swearing that we weren't there, that we were at Sarah's for the night."

Mason lays his head back against the headboard, staring at the ceiling. The despair and regret in those deep blue eyes show a man haunted by a child's memories. "I should've went out there. Done something. Instead, I cowered under the bed with the phone and called 911. The operator answered just in time to hear the gunshot."

Tears trail down his cheeks into his stubble, and my heart aches for him, for the little boy under the bed. I climb into his lap, wrapping my arms around his neck, and he runs his palms roughly over his face, embarrassed by his emotional response.

"Sweetheart," I murmur, running my fingers up and down the soft skin of his nape. "You did what she told you to do. She needed to know you were safe. How do you think she would've felt if you'd got between them and he'd hurt you, too. Or if you'd seen her get shot? Your mom loved you and did what was best for you. There's nothing you could've done for her, baby. You have to know that."

So many things about this man finally fall into place. He spends his life rescuing women from abusive relationships because he couldn't save the one he loved most, his mother.

His warm hands roam my back, drawing comfort from our connection and he drops a soft kiss on my lips before he continues. "I was too afraid to check on her, even after I heard the front door slam. I completely froze up. It took two cops to pull me from under the bed."

The shame and agony in his voice raise a lump in my throat. "You were ten years old, Mason, a boy. You were traumatized."

"Uncle Logan told me later there was nothing anyone could've done. He shot her in the head. She died instantly."

"I'm so sorry."

"I was so pissed at the system for failing her, failing us. Uncle Logan was irate as well, and he sued everyone involved on our behalf. Marion County, the cops, the judge, the state of Indiana. It was on the all the news networks for a year, and when it was over, the civil court jury awarded us with the unreal sum of ninety million dollars for wrongful death.

"Uncle Logan invested it for us and it grew even more by the time we were grown. It allowed me to start Striking Back, so at least something good came from all of it." His lips press together and he runs his fingers through my hair, gazing down at me. "Do you understand, love, why I started S.B.? And why I could never hurt a woman?"

"Yes," I whisper, resting my head on his shoulder. We're quiet for a minute before I ask, "Have you seen your father since?"

"Not since I testified against him." He shifts to lie down, taking me with him. "No more sharing tonight, okay? I'm done in."

"Okay. I love you. So much."

"Love you too, Panda."

His breathing evens out as he falls asleep, but I lay awake for over an hour, digesting all he's told me. We're both damaged, both trying to recover from horrific childhoods. What a depressing thing to have in common. I'm finally lulled to sleep by the comforting sound of his heartbeat beneath my ear.

Warm lips brush across my neck, making me smile before my eyes are open. "Good morning, sweetheart." His raspy morning voice is such a turn on.

"Mmm, are you going to make it one?" The heavy conversations we had last night were hard, but it's made me feel closer to him. He knows everything and—if the hands tugging off my panties are any indication—he still wants me.

I slide my hands up his abdomen, dragging my fingertips through his short, crisp chest hair. It only takes a second for our clothes to end up tangled on the floor. Mason practically dives on top of me, pinning my hands above my head with a low growl. My gasp causes him to hesitate, an anxious look on his face.

"Is this okay? I wouldn't have been so rough with you before if I'd known."

Shit. This is exactly what I was afraid of. "Hey." I look him in the eye. "I love how you fuck me. How dominating you can be, the dirty talk, all of it. You'll never be able to tell me what to do when I'm dressed so you better take advantage when I'm naked. Don't change a damn thing."

His slow wicked smile increases the moisture between my legs. "Then turn your sweet ass over, baby. I'm going to fuck you until you beg me to stop."

I barely have time to roll over when he grabs my hips and yanks me to the edge of the bed. Bent over at the foot of the bed, I can feel the heat of his body as he stands behind me, his hands squeezing my behind.

"I love your ass, Evie." His finger trails between my cheeks, stroking lightly over that forbidden place where no man has ever touched me. "Easy, love," he murmurs, kissing the dip in my lower back when I stiffen up.

"I've never…"

"No one has had your ass?" A deep groan echoes through the room when I shake my head. "You'll give it to me," he declares, his voice husky. "When you're ready."

"Fuck no! You aren't getting that beer can cock anywhere near my ass!"

He snorts with laughter and rubs his hot length between my cheeks. "We'll see." A thick finger dips inside me, quickly finding the spot that shuts off my brain. "You're dripping wet. Somebody missed me."

"Maybe I missed Little Mason." I'm squirming and pushing myself back on his fingers.

His hand connects sharply with my ass, and I cry out at the unexpected sting. "From beer can to little?"

"Mason Junior?" I suggest with a giggle. "What do you call it?"

"He who must be obeyed," he replies, burying himself up

to his balls and putting an end to my giggles.

I groan at the feel of that first wet stretch, and he grinds against me, delivering another slap on the lower curve of my cheek. "If you do that again, I'm going to come."

"Don't come until I say so," he orders. His words somehow shove me even closer to the edge.

"I can't stop it!"

"You'd better," he whispers in my ear. "Don't come." As soon as the words leave his lips, he surges into me hard and fast. He sets a ruthless pace, powering into me, his fingers digging into my hips. It takes all my concentration to resist my impending orgasm.

Maybe I'm crazy for fighting it, but I've never been able to pass up a challenge. He doesn't think I can do it, so I'm determined to hold out. A loud cry rips from my throat when his fingertip finds its target, rubbing small tight circles. "Mason!" I scream. I'm losing it, writhing and fisting the sheets.

"Come, Evie. Now." His firm command shoves me off the cliff, the world around me narrowing to a pinpoint where all that exists is devastating pleasure. Through the blissful haze, I feel his strong arm under my hips, supporting me when my legs turn to jelly.

When I find my way back to my brain, Mason's firm chest is draped across my back, his cock still throbbing inside me. His lips brush over my ear as he murmurs, "Good girl." I usually hate that phrase—it's something you'd say to a dog—but coming from him it doesn't sound demeaning. He's pleased with me, and I should be worried about how much that matters.

"Shit, Evie," he says as he pulls out. "I'm so sorry. I got carried away and didn't grab a condom."

"It's okay."

We crawl into bed, cuddling together. "Are you on birth control? Do we need to get a morning after pill?"

"We're covered, don't worry. I won't get pregnant and I'm clean."

He sighs with relief and runs his fingers through my hair. "I'm clean too. I can show you the test results if you want."

"That's not necessary. I trust you. I'm cool with ditching the condoms if you are."

I'm rewarded with a long soft kiss before he gazes into my eyes. "I love you."

"I love you."

"And taking your ass will be much easier without a condom." His crooked smile widens as I shake my head. "Never going to happen, Beer Can Cock."

"This Bud's for you."

"I can't believe you said that with a straight face."

We spend most of the day lounging around and enjoying one another's company. "It's a beautiful day. I should've brought a swimsuit so I could sunbathe," I remark. Mason's backyard is a mini paradise. A four foot deep in-ground pool stretches across the yard, surrounded by cushioned chaise lounges. A large cedar tree grows beside the patio, the canopy providing shade to a long stone picnic table.

"No one can see you through the privacy fence, love. You could lay out naked. Avoid those pesky tan lines."

"Dream on, buddy."

Mason disappears into his bedroom for a moment, returning with a black pair of boxer briefs. "These are too small for me. You can probably fit them."

The sun glints off the surface of the pool, calling to me. "Thanks." His eyes never leave me as I strip down to the bare and slip on his underwear. If I roll up the waistband, they aren't a bad fit.

When I pick up my bra, Mason grabs my hand. "No one will see those sweet tits but me. I'll be happy to cover them with sunblock."

Smiling, I shake my head. "You're incorrigible. Fine. I'll let the girls get some sun." I watch as Mason shoves two of the lounges together, his back flexing, biceps swelling, and a thin layer of sweat coating his skin. I can barely walk after our morning sex fest and still my body wants more. I'll never get enough of him.

His chuckle breaks my trance, and I realize I'm busted. He stalks toward me like a leopard on the hunt and grabs my ass with both hands. "Keep looking at me like that, Evie. See what comes of it."

"I'd come, I'm sure, but you've rode me raw. I'm too sore, so you'll just have to put that away." I glance down at the bulge in his shorts. "We're sunbathing, remember?"

"I'll be on my best behavior."

We lie side by side, talking about everything and nothing. We never seem to run out of things to talk about. After an hour on my stomach, I roll to my back, tucking my arms beneath my head. The sun feels fantastic, warming me inside and out, while a light breeze cools the sweat on my skin.

"Are you a sun worshipper?" Mason asks, amused.

"Guilty. I could do this all day."

"So could I." His eyes are fixed on my boobs, a cocky grin on his face.

"Best behavior," I remind him, giggling. We lie in comfortable silence for a while, and I'm just starting to doze when I feel his cool lips on my nipple.

He smiles when my breath catches, and leisurely licks my other nipple before sitting up and handing me a glass of ice water. "You fell asleep."

"Mmm, I was too comfortable."

He pulls our lounge chairs over a few feet so we're in the shade. "No burning the boobies."

I scoot closer to him, leaning against his sweaty chest. "I should visit Macy."

"I'll take you, then I'd like to take you out to dinner."

"Sounds great." I trace his tattoos with my fingertips, stopping just over his clavicle. "This isn't a scar."

"No."

"It's another flower."

"Mmm Hmm." He takes my finger and runs it along the border of the flower. "It's a white ink tattoo, a tulip."

Now that I'm close enough, I can see it clearly. "It's beautiful, but it's almost hidden."

"That one's just for me," he murmurs.

I press a soft kiss on his lips. "What does a white tulip represent?"

His hand slides into my hair and he tucks my head beneath his chin. "Forgiveness."

"Whose forgiveness do you need?"

"My own." I squeeze him around the waist, resting my head on his chest. After a few seconds of silence, I figure he's done talking about it, but he surprises me. "It took me years to forgive myself for not protecting my mom. I know she wouldn't have blamed me and whenever I struggle to remember that, I have the tattoo to remind me."

"I'm glad. I hate that you feel responsible for something that wasn't your fault."

"Ditto, baby," he replies, referring to my guilt over the abuse.

"We're quite a pair. Maybe I should get a tattoo."

"Just make sure it's something you want to always carry with you. That it has meaning."

"So no butterfly tramp stamp?" I tease, peeking up at him.

"How about my name on your ass?"

"And the deeper meaning behind that?"

His hand creeps beneath me. "This ass belongs to Mason. Plus, I'll be the only man to get inside it."

Laughing, I smack his chest. "Keep dreaming, Caveman."

After we clean up, Mason drives us to the hospital to visit Macy. She's propped up in bed watching television while Parker sits on a cot, tapping away on his laptop. "Ev," she says, grinning as her gaze falls to Mason's arm around my waist.

"Hey, Mace. How are you feeling?"

"A little better. They removed the chest tube so I might be able to go home tomorrow." Her face darkens at the word "home". She doesn't have a home right now. I can't imagine how awful that would feel when you're sick. When I was in the hospital, all I wanted was to go home, not to Mason's, but at least I knew I'd go home eventually.

Her reaction doesn't escape Parker's notice. "When you're discharged, we'll set you up in a safe house. It's a nice place and you can stay there as long as you need. You need to worry about getting better. Let us handle the rest."

"Thank you," Macy says softly, gazing at Parker with admiration.

"Let's give the ladies time to gossip," Mason suggests, dragging Parker into the hall.

"Are you back together?" Macy asks as soon as they've left the room.

"We are. It was all a big misunderstanding."

"I'm glad. He's obviously in love with you."

My head jerks to meet her gaze. "You think so?"

"It's all over his face, Ev. Like he doesn't know whether to worship you or fuck your brains out."

I grin at her. "He manages both at once."

"Don't you dare screw this up, girl." She wags a finger at me.

"I'm trying not to." The next hour passes quickly while we chat and laugh together. She's thrilled with the trilogy of new romance books and chocolate I've brought her. When she starts to look tired, I text Mason and give her a hug, promising to see her again soon.

On the drive home, Mason announces his plan to have a small pool party on the Fourth of July. "Invite Ian if you'd like," he offers.

"I will. I wish Amy could come. I miss her, but she's happy in New York. Oh! I have to take the BTC kids to the fireworks that evening."

"We'll celebrate early."

"Sounds fun."

Chapter Five

Evie

July fourth dawns bright and sunny, perfect for Mason's pool party. Alex and Cooper show up first, followed by Ian, Parker, and Macy. "Hey, Everly!" Alex smiles and hugs me. "It's so good to see you."

"You, too. I was starting to forget what you look like," I tease.

Alex slides an arm around Cooper with a grin. "Sorry, I've been…occupied."

"So this is your fault," I tease, giving Cooper a quick hug.

A dimple dents his cheek. "I'd like to say I'm sorry, but…" He shrugs. They are just too damn cute together.

"Are we eating or what?" Parker demands, barging into the kitchen.

"Ugh, you have all the grace of a rhino." I poke him in the side.

"Got other rhino parts, too," he replies with a cocky grin.

A squeal echoes through the house, and I'm caught up in a tight hug. "Bitch, I missed you!" Amy cries, crushing my ribs.

"Amy? What the hell? What are you doing here?"

"Your tatted Adonis flew me out for the weekend." We squeal and hug again. Damn, I've missed her.

Mason turns to me with a smug grin. "Tatted Adonis?"

Great, add to his already swollen head. "Shut up." I smack his chest before kissing him hard. "I can't believe you did this!"

"You said you missed her, and I wanted to surprise you."

"You did. Thank you." Hugging him, I whisper in his ear. "I'm going to suck you so good, later."

"Christ, Evie," he moans, and Amy laughs.

"Bet I can guess what you promised him," she teases.

"And that's our cue to head out back," Alex says with a chuckle.

"Head being the key word," Parker quips.

I feel my cheeks heat and excuse myself to go change into my swimsuit. "So," Mason says, leading Amy out to the back patio. "Evie called me a tatted Adonis?" I hear everyone laugh and can't help the smile on my face. My friends and the man I love are here. Today is going to be fun.

Macy, Amy, and I relax in lounge chairs by the pool, soaking in the sun while the guys hang out by the grill. "What is it about guys and a barbecue?" Amy scoffs, gesturing in their direction.

"What do you think they're talking about?" Macy asks.

"Let's read their lips," I suggest with a giggle.

"Flip that steak," Macy mocks in a deep voice.

Parker points to the grill and I put words into his mouth. "No! Flip the other one!"

Amy shakes her head at us. "Not even close. Look at Mason." She drops her voice into a growl. "Evie's going to suck my cock dry."

"Amy!" I smack her arm, and we all laugh, drawing the guys' attention.

"Come on, Ev. Tell me his cock is as magnificent as the rest of him. It's huge, isn't it?"

Glancing at Mason, I give him a wink and spread my hands seven or eight inches apart. "Massive." Smirking, he shakes his head at me, well aware we're talking about him.

A wall of water douses us, and when I sweep the drops from my eyes, I see Parker grinning at us, his elbows resting on the edge of the pool. "Asshole," Amy splutters. "What the hell are you doing?"

"At the moment I'm fighting the urge to make you the happiest woman on earth tonight." His lust filled eyes rake over Amy's bikini clad body.

"Somebody didn't get the memo," Macy whispers.

"Forget it, Parker. You're barking up the wrong vagina," I call.

"You're supposed to put a good word in for me with your friends, Ev," Parker replies, pretending to be offended.

"Sorry, you're not my type, handsome."

"Handsome isn't your type? How about very well-endowed?"

"Well-endowed tits, maybe," I mumble, and we laugh.

"Don't make me whip it out and prove it, ladies."

"Unless you can whip out a nice smooth, tight vagina, I'm not interested."

Understanding dawns on his face, but he's only rattled for a second. "Fuck, that's hot. So have you and Evie?"

A sunscreen tube and water bottle fly at his head, interrupting his question. "All right!" He gives another killer smile before swimming off. "Just a suggestion."

"What a pig." Amy laughs, turning onto her stomach.

"Yeah, he's a good guy, though," I remark.

"He is," Macy adds softly. "He stayed with me in the hospital and he's been at the safe house since I moved there."

"How are you feeling, Mace?"

"Better." She sighs. "Physically anyway. I'm having panic attacks and anxiety. Then I get pissed off because I never had those issues before Al's bullshit."

I reach to squeeze her hand. "It'll get better. I wish there was something I could do."

"You introduced me to Striking Back. I don't know what I'd have done without their support. I'll feel better when he's locked up, though."

"They'll find him. If there's one thing I've learned about the Reed brothers, it's that they're relentless and stubborn."

"No wonder you and Mason bump heads," Amy snorts, and

I have to laugh.

I shift to lie on my stomach, my chin propped on my arm as I look around me. Mason and Parker are relaxing on the patio while Alex, Cooper, and Ian throw a football around. I get that wonderful warm feeling again that I imagine people feel when they're around family.

I love my friends and Mason. They feel like family, and damned if I'm not starting to feel the same about Alex and Parker. I remember Parker saying, "You're one of us, now," after I was nearly drowned. It feels good to be one of them.

It's one of the best afternoons I've had in a long time. Everyone gathers around the picnic table, eating and talking. Ian really seems to hit it off with Alex and Cooper, and they head off to Mason's garage to play pool. Parker and Mason beat Amy and me in a hilarious game of volleyball in the pool.

"Never had a chance!" Mason taunts, pinning me against the edge of the pool by my hips. His warm tongue slips between my lips, exploring and sending shivers through me.

"Of resisting you? Obviously not." A groan rattles his chest when I slide my hand over the front of his shorts. "Hmm, isn't it supposed to shrink in cold water? I don't think Longfellow here got the message."

"Longfellow?" I'm rewarded with a crooked grin before he runs his tongue up the side of my neck.

"Do you have a better name?"

"Hmm, how about All Day Sucker?"

"Let's go find out." I grab his hand and lead him up the stone steps from the pool. Amy, Macy, and Parker hoot as we head into the house, and I flip them off without looking back. My mind is focused on the dripping wet perfection beside me.

A low sexy chuckle just makes me move faster, yanking him into his bedroom and kicking the door shut. My hands slide under his waistband, and I drop to my knees taking his board shorts down as I go. The hiss of air he draws through clenched teeth when I suck him in makes me smile. I'm going to wreck him.

"Evie...fuck," he groans, his hands threading into my hair. I tease him, licking every hard inch before taking him in again.

He's so damn wide, my jaw aches, but I barely notice. My senses are full of him. I inhale his natural musky scent mixed with chlorine, my hands wandering around to squeeze his firm ass. "Oh…so good…fuck." His words come in small bursts between gasps and groans. "I'm close, Evie," he warns.

That's my cue to slide two wet fingers just behind his balls and deliver two firm strokes in the right spot. A cross between a shout and a yelp fills the room as he fills my throat. I look up at him, thoroughly satisfied with what I see. He's leaning against the wall, head tilted back, chest rising and falling as he pants, trying to pull himself together.

I pull his shorts back up, leaving them hang on his hips so I can lick each side of that sexy V. A strong hand grabs my nape when I stand and the other clamps almost painfully on my ass as he slams his lips on mine. He kisses me long and hard with no reservations about where my mouth has been. I love it that he doesn't care. That he can be dirty.

When we come up for air, our gazes lock, and the vulnerability in his eyes peels away the protective layer I've wrapped around my feelings. Who am I kidding? He's burrowed through and crawled into my heart for good. "You break me into pieces, Everly."

I wrap my arms around his warm back, and he embraces me. "And you put me back together."

We stay there for a moment, wrapped up in one another. My eyes close when his lips land on my forehead, lingering affectionately. The moment is broken when a cacophony of voices shakes the house. "Guess someone got hustled at the pool table," Mason remarks, shaking his head.

"We'd better go check on the kids," I reply, laughing.

It's early evening when the party breaks up. Amy and I make plans to get together again before she flies back to New York. Ian leaves with Cooper and Alex to hit the bars and continue their quest to get trashed.

Parker slaps Mason on the back. "I'd better get Macy back to the safe house." He turns and gives me an unexpected hug. "It was good to see you, Ev. When you get tired of old ugly here, give me a call. I promise not to chain you up."

Christ, does everyone know? I smack Parker on the chest before sliding my arms around Mason's waist. "I prefer my captors dark and handsome."

"Well, when it's dark, he's handsome." Parker laughs, dodging Mason's hand when it flies toward the back of his head.

"Come and visit, Ev, if you can," Macy pleads. "I'm going crazy being cooped up."

"Definitely. I need a girl's night," I reply, hugging her before they leave.

The house seems so quiet as Mason grins down at me. "Did you have fun?"

"I did. I think I need a shower and a nap before we go to the fireworks, though." Goosebumps race across my skin when he grips my hips from behind and nuzzles my neck.

"Want some company in the shower?" His warm breath tickles my ear.

"Can you keep your hands to yourself?"

"Hell no."

"We'd better hurry, then."

♥

I've volunteered to chaperone the BTC trip to the bank of White River for the big fireworks display. The city sponsors it every year and they go all out. I told Mason he didn't have to accompany me, that he could go hang out with his buddies, but he insists. Needless to say, I'm terribly disappointed with his decision.

After a quickie in the shower and an hour long nap, we set off to BTC. The kids are running around like lunatics, excited about the trip. Matty spots Mason and runs to meet us. "I'm in Mason's group!" he cries, attaching himself to Mason's leg.

Laughing, Mason scoops him up, shifting him onto his back where he clings like a chimp. "You'll have to ask Everly."

I ruffle Matty's hair. "Let me go talk to the counselors and see how we're dividing up."

We end up with Matty, Justin—another eight year old—and James, our fifteen year old resident smartass. We'll all be meeting at the river, but each counselor or volunteer is responsible for their own group of kids.

"I'm too old for fireworks," James grumbles, buckling his seatbelt.

"Are you too old for girls in tank tops and short shorts?" Mason asks with a smirk. "Cause there will be a lot of them at the river."

I smack Mason as James replies, "Proceed."

We find an empty spot on the wide riverbank and lay out a couple of blankets. Matty takes Mason's hand as we walk to the edge of the river. "Can I get wet?" Justin asks.

"If you want to grow a third testicle," James quips.

Justin's eyes widen. "Screw that." This boy has been spending too much time with James.

"It's too dirty, Justin. You could get sick from swimming in it. See there?" I point to a spot along the shore where the water is thick with soggy food wrappers, soda cans, and other refuse.

"It smells bad too," Matty says, waving a hand in front of his nose.

"Come with me. I want to show you something before it gets dark." I lead them up the embankment and to the middle of the Sixteenth Street Bridge which has been closed to traffic. "Look down, just beside that stone piling."

They all lean against the guardrail and peer over the side. "A car!" Matty cries. "How did it get there?"

"It's been there since I was a kid. I guess there was a crash and it went off the bridge."

"Awesome," James says. "I bet there's a rotting skeleton in it. Maybe more than one."

Justin looks up at me, his face stricken. "There are no skeletons," I assure him.

"Cause police would rescue them when they crashed, right?"

"That's right," Mason reassures him, shaking his head at James. It gets dark fast and we head back down to the riverbank where vendors are hocking t-shirts, novelties, and food.

"Can we get an ice cream?" Matty asks.

Mason buys the boys an ice cream while James and I decide on elephant ears. I sit on the grass between Justin and Matty. As they chatter away, I strain to hear Mason and James conversation behind us.

"Real?" James says doubtfully.

"Fake," Mason replies. "See how close together they are? Dead giveaway." Oh, they are not talking about breasts! Mason winks at me when I look back at him.

James points to a woman bouncing past in a bikini top. "Fake?"

"Good eye. They're too perfectly round, like cantaloupes."

"Damn big cantaloupes." James laughs.

"You two are disgusting," I inform them, trying not to crack a smile. At least James is interested in something.

When I turn back around James murmurs, "I'll bet Ev's are real." My shoulders shake with laughter when James remark is followed by the sound of Mason slapping him on the back of the head.

We head back to the BTC group and settle on our blankets just as the fireworks begin. Matty and Justin sit on a blanket in front of ours, eyes glued to the glittering sky. Mason nods at James, who wanders a few feet away to sit with a girl from his school.

"You're a bad influence," I tease, sitting cross legged between Mason's knees.

"Aw, the boy's in love. I know how he feels." I close my eyes as his lips tenderly touch my neck.

A joy and contentment like I've never known swells within me as I lean back against his chest. The air is thick with music and laughter, peppered with the deep thunder of fireworks, and redolent with the scent of fried dough and popcorn. Wonder filled faces gaze skyward, illuminated with shifting color, eyes shining and happy.

"You're smiling like you have a secret," Mason murmurs.

"No secret. I'm just…happy to be here in your arms. To spend the holiday with someone who loves me."

"We'll have many more holidays together, sweetheart."

If I have one wish tonight, he just nailed it.

Chapter Six

Mason

A phone ringing in the middle of the night is never good news. Evie's warm body is wrapped around mine as I reach for my cell. Sometimes, my girl could sleep through a hurricane. Officer Jack Robert's name flashes on the screen.

"Jack?"

"Mason. I'm sorry to call you so late, but I got a situation. A woman and baby that need to be anywhere else but here."

"Text me the address."

"The quicker the better, Reed. Before the detectives show up."

I realize Jack is sticking his neck out on this one. It won't be the first time we teamed up to help an abused woman out of a house before charges can be filed. This is what we do. I'm lucky to have amassed a caring group of cops, lawyers, judges, and paramedics willing to put their asses on the line to help these women. Women who have been abused for years would end up in jail for what is essentially self-defense if it weren't for these allies.

Evie's sleepy eyes regard me when I sit up and pull on my jeans. "What's wrong?"

"Someone needs my help." After considering it for a second, I brush her hair from her cheek, and ask, "Come with me?" She's out of bed and dressed in a matter of seconds.

The night air is cool on my arms, and I see Evie give a little shiver as we hop in the car. Fortunately, the address is close. I hand Evie my phone. "Dial Devon Hughes and put it on speaker."

"Hughes," he answers.

"Devon, I need a guy at Blue House."

"You got me. An hour at most."

Evie gazes at me after he hangs up. "Can you tell me where we're going?"

"We're going to get a woman and baby out of a bad situation and relocate them. I don't know exactly what we're walking into, but there shouldn't be any danger. Maybe I'm crazy for asking you to come, but after our past misunderstandings, I want you to see what I do."

Her soft hand lands on my knee. "I'm glad you brought me. I told you I want to play a bigger part in Striking Back."

"I know, but if you see or hear anything…if it's too much, promise you'll tell me, or come back to the car."

"I promise, but I can handle it."

"I don't doubt you can, love." She smiles when I grin at her. After all she's been through, her strength is inspiring.

Two police cars and an ambulance are parked haphazardly in the road, lights flashing. It's an ominous sight that never fails to trigger bad memories. Especially if it's raining, like the night the police led me away from the house where my mother died.

Evie is right behind me when I walk through the front door of a tiny brick home. Blood puddles on the floor surrounding a large man wearing only boxers. Paramedics crouch over him, trying to stop his beer gut from bleeding. Jack nods at me and gestures toward the back of the house. "She's in the kitchen with my partner."

I note that both medics are familiar and know how to play the game. "Get her gone. Work on her story. This asshole walked right into a knife," Jack says. Nodding, I take Evie's hand and we make our way to the kitchen.

A wide eyed woman streaked with blood sits on the floor, leaning against the cabinet. "I stabbed him," she chants. "I stabbed him. I'll go to jail…and Jesse…they'll take my baby." Jack's partner is trying to console her and advise her what to say.

"No, dear. He walked into the knife. You weren't even here."

"The baby…Jesse," she whimpers.

I have to swallow back my anger at the sight of the tiny blond woman. She can't weigh over one-hundred pounds soaking wet. That asshole could've broken her in half. She cringes as I approach her, and I try to soften my voice. "Miss, I'm here to bring you and your baby to a safe place where your husband can't find you. You need to get the baby and come with us." She's in shock, and I can see my message isn't getting through. She buries her face in her hands, sobbing.

Evie doesn't hesitate. She sits beside her, hip to hip, mindless of the blood. "What's your name, honey?" she asks quietly.

"Jenny," she replies between sobs.

"I'm Everly. I know you're scared and confused, but I need you to listen to me. Do you want to help your baby?"

That makes Jenny pause. "Yes, of course."

"Good. See the man in the red shirt? He runs a shelter for abused women and children. The policeman let us know you need help and that's why we're here. Do you understand?" Evie takes the woman's trembling hand.

"Yes."

"Then I need you to go pack a bag for you and your baby. Right now. Just grab the necessities, we can get you whatever else you need. But you need to be quick. Can you do that? I'll help you."

Jenny nods and gets to her feet, leading Everly to the bedroom. After they leave, I turn to see Jack standing in the doorway. "Is she new?"

"She's worked at the main shelter for a while."

"She's good, a natural. Don't let that one go."

"I don't intend to." I'm awed by how Evie handled the situation, like she's done it a hundred times. They return with a small suitcase and diaper bag. Jenny grips the handle of a safety seat, where a baby lies sleeping, covered in a blue blanket.

When we emerge from the house the medics are loading

the injured husband into the ambulance. A steady stream of profanity and threats pour from his mouth at the sight of his wife. "No worries, ma'am," the medic calls. "Idiot ran himself into a knife. Told me and my partner all about it." His partner nods and understanding begins to dawn in Jenny's eyes.

"We have to go," I warn, leading her to the car. She buckles the safety seat in the back and climbs in.

After about ten minutes, she asks, "Where are you taking us?"

"To a safe house. It's furnished and stocked with food and necessities. You'll have a security guard with you just in case, but by the looks of your husband, he'll be in the hospital for a while, anyway. Do you have a cell phone?"

"Yes."

I reach into the console and produce a pre-paid cell phone. "Transfer whatever numbers you need to this phone now, then turn yours off and remove the SIM card. You need to be off grid for a bit until everything blows over."

"I can't believe this is happening," she murmurs, following my instructions.

"I know it's scary," Evie says. "Not knowing where you're going or what's going to happen. But you'll be safe. Your boy will be safe."

Jenny nods. "Do you have children?" she asks.

"No," Evie replies, "but I work with kids."

"You should. You'd be a good mother."

Everly flinches before covering her response with a smile. "Thank you."

"We have about an hour drive, ladies. Does anyone need anything? Bathroom?"

"I'm okay," Jenny replies, and Everly shakes her head. I don't know if she has something on her mind, or if all this is catching up with her, but she's quiet throughout the rest of the trip, a pensive look on her face as she gazes out the window. We'll have plenty to discuss later, but for now, I'm fiercely proud of my girl and the way she handled things tonight.

Jack calls to let me know we're in the clear. The official

police report says her husband got drunk and walked into a knife. With only a single stab wound, it appears the man will live.

Devon's jeep is parked in the driveway of Blue House when we arrive. We use code names when discussing the safe houses, and this one is named for its deep navy blue color. Jenny looks like she may collapse from exhaustion as she unfastens the baby's safety seat.

"Let me carry him," Evie offers. She's never looked more awake, her eyes alive with the excitement of the night. I remember feeling that way in the beginning, getting that adrenaline rush. Jenny hands the baby seat over with a grateful look. I grab her bags, and they follow me inside the modest two bedroom home.

"The bedroom on the right is yours," I inform her. "There's an attached bath. Make yourself at home."

"I'll help you get unpacked and settled," Evie says, escorting her to the bedroom.

"What's the story?" Devon asks.

"Stabbed the abusive husband. Medics think he'll live. She won't if he finds her, though. We need one man here while the husband's still in the hospital. Add an outside guard once he's released. Twelve hour shifts."

"Are cops going to be looking for her?"

"No, Jack Roberts caught the case. She wasn't even home tonight. Guy walked into his own knife."

"She only stick him once?"

"Yeah."

"Should hold up then." Devon slides a cup of coffee across the table. "I can get my sister to run to the store, get whatever she needs for the kid."

"I'll handle it," Evie says, stalking past and giving Devon a look that would shrink the testicles of a lesser man. Ignoring his smirk, she turns to me. "I need a pen and paper."

"Desk drawer in the living room."

"Thanks." She's all business as she settles on the couch with Jenny to make a list of necessary items.

The dining room and living room are all one open area, but

Devon and I pretend we aren't listening to them as we sit at the dining table. "Your girl hasn't forgiven me for that needle," Devon says with an amused expression.

"Not sure I'm off the shit list for that either," I reply. It's funny watching Evie glare at Devon, not the least bit intimidated by his hulking size or fierce expression.

Jenny bursts into tears, and Evie embraces her. "It's not too much. We get plenty of donations and this is how we use them to help."

"By buying panties and pacifiers?" Jenny asks with a snort. They look at each other and dissolve into giggles. "Well, a girl's got to have panties."

"Go grab a shower and try to get some rest before Jesse wakes. You'll feel better. It's hard to think with no sleep." Jenny hugs her again and heads off toward the bedroom.

"She's a good one," Devon remarks as Evie approaches us.

"Is there a Superstore nearby?"

"Not too far. I'll take you when you're ready." Doubt clouds her face at the thought of leaving Jenny with Devon. Taking her hand, I lead her to the spare bedroom. "I know you don't like him, Panda, but this is what he does, the same as me. He's here to protect Jenny. He'd never hurt her. You need to remember I had you drugged and brought back. It wasn't his call."

"Fine. Let's go."

Devon sits on the couch and flips on the television as we walk by. "You'll be happy to know my toes are no longer taped together," he tells Evie, who gives him a perplexed look. "Two broken toes," he explains, "had to be taped together until they healed. May never be back to normal, though." He can't prevent a mischievous grin from sneaking across his face.

I see the corner of Evie's mouth twitch as she tries not to smile. "Left foot, wasn't it?"

"Yep."

"So, I know the weak spot to aim for next time."

Devon's deep laughter follows us out the door.

We return to find Jenny fast asleep and Jesse just beginning to stir. Evie scoops up the baby, shutting the bedroom door behind her so Jenny can sleep. "She's exhausted. I'll look after Jesse for a few hours."

"I have to go to Striking Back. We can come back this evening and check on them if you like."

She looks up at me, and I tuck a stray lock of hair behind her ear. "I'm safe here with your goon, aren't I?"

"I heard that, devil woman," Devon calls from the kitchen.

Evie grins as she changes Jesse's diaper, and the baby smiles back at her. "Goons have good hearing."

"Little devil," Devon mutters good naturedly.

"Can you just pick me up this evening?"

"Are you sure? I know you're tired."

"I'm fine. Go handle your end and let me help here." With Jesse cradled in the crook of her arm, she heats up his formula in a pan of hot water.

"Call me if you change your mind, then. Or tell Devon. I can send someone to come get you. You can't tell Ian or Amy where you are."

"Duh. Quit worrying. I'll be fine." She drops a quick kiss on my lips.

"I'll be back by six."

I replay the night's events in my head during the drive back to Indy. Evie couldn't have done a better job with Jenny, and is going above and beyond to help them today. The gleam in her eye and bounce in her step betray her happiness. Her bravery and compassion, that fearless and caring nature…she was born for this. And it only magnifies my love and admiration for this stubborn woman.

If I didn't think she'd run screaming, I'd propose today. I can't make her mine right now, but I can pave the way. I pull into a fast food drive through to grab some breakfast and call my lawyer. "Landon, tell me some good news."

"They accepted your offer and the zoning has been cleared. You can break ground at your leisure."

"That's what I wanted to hear. I also need to add a name to the account. She should have full access to the funds."

"You finally hire a CFO?"

"Something like that. I'll email you the info."

"Do that. I have some forms you need to sign."

"I'll be in my office today if you want to messenger them."

"Anything else you need right now?"

"Two more of me, and another of you. Anyone perfect cloning yet?"

"I'm one of a kind, asshole. When's the next poker night?"

"I'll take your money soon. Thanks, Landon."

"Anytime."

My day is boring compared to the previous night. Money has to grease a lot of palms to keep things running right and that means we're always looking for ways to raise funds. I really do need to hire someone to deal with that facet of the business. Maybe Evie has some fundraising ideas.

I work my way through a ton of emails and fill out a stack of paperwork before heading downstairs to speak to Ms. Den. She assures me everything is running smoothly with no issues since Macy's attack. Finally, I can head back to Everly.

When I approach Blue House I hear Everly shout, "Bullshit!"

Instantly on edge, I dart inside to find Evie, Devon, and Jenny playing cards while the baby crawls around the room. "Reed, your woman cheats," Devon growls, gathering together a pile of cards.

Evie beams up at me. "He's just mad because he can't beat me."

"It's a ridiculous game," Devon scoffs.

"What are you playing?" I ask, taking Evie's hand and pulling her to her feet.

"Bullshit. It's not much fun with only three people. I'll teach you some time. You ready to go?"

"Will you stay with me tonight?"

"Aren't you getting sick of me yet?" Her soft lips find mine for a brief kiss. She'll know soon that I want her with me every night.

"Never, love. Let's go."

Jenny hugs Evie. "Thanks for everything, Ev."

"Hang in there. You can do this," Evie assures her. "Call anytime."

"Later, Goon," Evie calls to Devon over her shoulder as we go.

"Take care, Devil Woman."

Evie smiles at me across the breakfast table and even after nailing her to the bed and making her scream in the shower, I get hard again. I swear I could spend my life fucking this woman. No one has ever affected me the way she does. "Do you have plans today?"

"I haven't been home in a while. I should probably visit my apartment. Make sure it's still standing."

"We can stay at your place tonight if you like, but I want to take you somewhere today."

"So mysterious," she coos. "Where?"

"To show you something."

"That's all you're going to tell me?"

"Yep."

Chapter Seven

Evie

Mason stays close lipped the entire ride to wherever the hell we're going. We've been driving for over an hour, and I feel a little nervous as he turns onto a narrow paved road. I've watched him grow more excited as the city fell behind us and the trees and fields began to fill the landscape.

He's thrilled to show me something, and I don't want to disappoint him with the wrong reaction. If only I had a clue what was coming. Things have been great since we reunited. We spend every night together and most days as well. I still spend a couple of days a week at Building Tomorrow's Child, but most of my time is focused on Striking Back as Mason shows me more and more about how his operation works.

The narrow road widens, ending in a cracked circular driveway. A walkway made of smooth stones leads to a beautiful two story house. Painted the blue of a robin's egg with white trim, it seems to radiate the peace and tranquility of the woods and fields surrounding it.

"Who lives here?" I ask as Mason takes my hand and leads me around the back of the house.

"No one yet." He gestures to the fields behind the house that seem to stretch for miles. "I just closed on this property. You're looking at the future site of Striking Back, a long term housing option for recovering women and their children.

A proud grin settles on his face as he points to two bulldozers working at the top of a hill in the distance. "That's where the apartments will be located."

"This is amazing. Just fantastic," I exclaim.

"It'll be for women like Jenny. Relocating to another state where they know no one and have no support system isn't what's best for them or their children. They can live here in their own apartment, but alongside other women and children in their situation. We can help them go back to school or find a job, provide transportation and childcare until they're able to make it on their own."

Is it any wonder I fell so hard for this man? I never had a damn chance. He leads me back to the front porch as he talks, and we sit on the steps. "The house needs very little work, although I'm not thrilled with some of the wallpaper. Looks like an eighty year old woman lived here. Not exactly manly."

Heaviness fills my chest. "You plan to live here? It'll be a long commute to Striking Back," I point out. And a long way from me.

"I'm moving SB to here. The shelter downtown just isn't large or secure enough."

I force a smile. "It's a beautiful place. Perfect surroundings for healing and a great place for kids."

His large palms cup my jaws and his gaze is intense as it meets mine. "I want you with me, Evie. Live here with me."

All my breath flees my body. He couldn't have surprised me more if he'd asked for me to get naked and do the chicken dance. When did it get so damn hot out here? Live with him? Did Mason just ask me to move in with him? "I…don't you think it's a little soon?"

"I don't care. I want you wrapped around me every night and smiling at me across the breakfast table every morning."

Oh god. He can't do this to me. How can I resist him when he says things like that? Things are going so well. What if this screws up our relationship? "Breathe, love." Soft fingertips stroke my cheek. "You don't have to decide now. Take some time to think about it."

"I'm sorry, I…it's not that I don't want to. I love you. I love being with you. I've seen what it's like to lose you. If I screw this up…" A lump rises in my throat and I swallow back tears at the thought. "I can't lose you again."

Strong arms embrace me. "I'm not going anywhere. If you aren't ready to live together, I'll understand. I can wait. You'll come around eventually," he teases. "You know you can't resist me."

"Cocky," I reply with a laugh.

"Don't say cock or I'll have to break in the bedroom before there's a bed. Come on." He gets to his feet and takes my hand. "Let me show you what you'll be getting other than a live-in tatted Adonis sex god."

He grins at my snort. "I don't remember calling you a sex god."

"I saw it in your eyes."

"Oh yeah." I gaze at him. "What are my eyes saying now?"

His forehead rests against mine, and those bright blues bore into me. His feigned shocked expression makes me giggle. "Oh! Such filthy thoughts in those beautiful eyes. You've corrupted me! I'm corrupted!"

I smack his ass as he rubs his eyes with balled fists. I know what he's doing, trying to break the tension and let me off the hook for getting upset at his request. He always makes me feel better. I can't imagine my life without him, so why am I fighting this?

He leads me through the house, and I try to picture living here with him. It's a gorgeous place, four bedrooms with adjoining baths, a large modern kitchen, and a formal dining room. But it's the large room across from the master bedroom that really makes me want to move in tomorrow.

Bookshelves line three walls, while the fourth features a wide fireplace. Thick chocolate colored carpet is soft beneath my feet and I want to strip off my shoes and sink my toes in it. "Do you like the den?" Mason asks. "We could pull up the carpet, expose the hardwood like the rest of the house."

"Don't you dare," I breathe. His eyebrows reach for the ceiling—where there's a skylight, I might add—and he grins. "It's a perfect library." I can picture curling up on a soft sofa with one of my favorite books, a fire crackling in the fireplace.

"Do you like the place?" he asks, guiding me back downstairs.

"I love it." I stop him when we get to the car and take both his hands in mine. I know he was so excited to bring me here and hopeful my answer would be yes. I've disappointed him and it makes me feel terrible. If he only knew how badly I want to say yes.

"I can see myself living here with you. I want to. I want you…but…I'm afraid. There's so much that could go wrong, so much we'd need to work out."

He releases my hands and slides his hands behind my neck, stroking my nape. "Just the fact that you admitted you're scared, that you told me how you feel, shows how far we've come. We can make it work if we're honest with each other. Let's go get some lunch and talk about it."

"Okay."

Mason stops at an IHOP on our way home, and I groan as we settle into a booth, facing each other. "You're killing me. I can't eat here without having the French toast. My ass is going to be so fat you'll have to pry me from the booth."

"Baby, your ass could never be too big."

"Good to know, huh?" I ask the grinning waitress standing behind him.

"Sorry," he says, sounding anything but. She takes our order and hurries away. After a few seconds of silence, he asks, "What concerns you most about moving in together?"

I fiddle with the tiny box of crayons placed on the table alongside a children's paper placemat. My deepest fear is once he spends too much time with me, he'll see who I really am and realize he doesn't love me. It's happened with every set of foster parents and with my only serious relationship. "What if you don't like living with me? If you're unhappy, our relationship will fall apart."

"Why wouldn't I like living with you?"

"I'm messy." I blurt the first thing that comes to mind.

His deep laughter makes it hard not to smile. "We'll get a housekeeper. I'm not exactly neat."

"I can be a real bitch sometimes," I warn.

"Really? I hadn't noticed." Amusement is clear in his voice.

"I'm serious."

"You mean like when you're hungry or cold or haven't had enough sleep?" he teases. Damn. Maybe he does know me. "I'll feed you, wrap you in a blanket, and put you to bed. After I make you come to improve your mood." I can't help but giggle. I'm running out of excuses. "This is all trivial. You want to know what I think you're scared of?"

"Please, enlighten me."

"Being in love. It makes you vulnerable to being hurt again, but it's too late for that, Panda. We're in love whether we live together or not." His warm hands close over mine. "I won't hurt you, Evie. I swear on my brothers, I'll always be there for you. Right beside you."

Damn it. He's going to make me cry in public. "You're too damn good to be true, Mason Reed," I choke. "I love you. I promise to be there when you need me. If you're beside me, I'm beside you. Always."

A gorgeous smile spreads across his face. "You'll move in with me?"

"Yes."

Leaping to his feet, he rounds the table and slides into the seat beside me. I'm smothered in nearly two hundred pounds of ecstatic—and apparently turned on—male. His lips are at my ear. "I'm going to eat you for hours tonight."

"You'll get no argument from me."

"Now." He turns the children's placemat over to the blank side and grabs a blue crayon. "Let's put it in writing."

"What are you doing?" I giggle as he scribbles away. When he leans back, I can see what he's written.

Mason Reed and Everly Hall do hereby agree to the following:

1. To love one another for eternity.

2. To have amazing, dirty, kinky, mind blowing sex as often as Evie's vagina can handle.

I grab the crayon to add my own promises:

3. To touch only one another's genitals and kiss only each other's lips.

4. To be honest and keep no secrets.

The crayon is plucked from my fingers and he adds to the list:

5. To talk about our problems instead of running or hiding.

6. To never ask Mason to buy feminine products.

7. To protect and guard Everly with my life.

I'm still laughing over number six when he hands me the crayon. I draw a line through number seven and write:

7. To protect and guard each other with our lives.

8. To never use the same knife in the peanut butter and jelly jars.

Mason adds:

9. To remain right beside Everly.

I add:

10. To remain right beside Mason.

I sign and date the bottom, and Mason adds his signature. "We're keeping this," he warns.

"It's ironclad," I reply.

"Wait! I forgot to add in the part about anal. I'm entitled to claim your ass." The waitress can't suppress her giggle this time. He really has the worst timing.

Chapter Eight

Mason

A knock at the door interrupts our breakfast. "Are you expecting your brothers?" Evie asks.

"No, but that never stops them." Evie follows me to the front door. When I open it, the last person I want to see is on the other side. Jamie Weldow. "What the fuck are you doing here?" I demand, before noticing the skinny little boy standing beside her.

She smirks. "Nice to see you too." A hateful grin tilts her lips. "I thought it was time you met your son."

Her words are worse than any choke hold and my chest tightens painfully. She's lying. She has to be. I only fucked her a couple of times and never without a condom. Lying fucking bitch.

Before I can tell her where to go, Evie's hand lands on my shoulder. "Maybe you should talk about this in private." She regards Jamie stone faced, and I know she's shocked, trying to hold it together and make things easier on the kid. Great. Another thing to send her running. "Is it okay if your son joins me in the kitchen while you two talk?"

Jamie's eyes scan Everly, and she frowns. "Whatever. Take him. Cody, go with her."

Disapproval is written on Evie's face at her callous order. She kneels in front of the small boy, and he stares at the floor, shuffling his feet. "Hi, Cody. My name is Everly. I like your t-shirt."

A small smile emerges as he peeks up at her. "He's the Incredible Hulk. He smashes bad guys."

"He's awesome. Will you come and tell me more about him?" Nodding, he puts his hand in hers and allows her to lead him away.

Jamie huffs as I step out onto the porch instead of inviting her inside. I seriously need to get downwind. Judging by her greasy hair and stained clothes, she hasn't had an acquaintance with a bar of soap for a while. "That's how you're going to treat the mother of your child?"

"You know damn well that kid isn't mine. What kind of shit are you trying to pull?"

"He's yours and I'm tired of taking care of him alone."

"How old is he?" I ask, desperately trying to remember the last time I fucked her.

"Five." Shit. That doesn't rule it out.

"You realize I can get a DNA test?"

"So do it." She sits on the step for a moment only to get right back to her feet. I recognize her fidgeting for what it is. Withdrawal. Six years hasn't changed her.

"You're jonesing. Is that what this is about? You want money so you can drag that poor kid around with you while you shoot up?"

The eyes of a predator stare hatefully at me. "Fuck you. I'm not using. You owe me for years of child support." She glances around her. "It's not like you can't afford it."

"There's no fucking way I'm giving you money for drugs and letting you leave with that boy." I suppose there's a small chance he's mine, but blood or not, he's not being left in this situation.

"So keep him."

Her blunt answer catches me off guard, and I stare at her in amazement. "What?"

Realizing she pissed me off, she starts backpedaling. "Not…you know…for good. Just a few hours while I find us a place to stay. I'll come pick him up, but I need money for a room."

Fuck fuck fuck. Fine. I want her as far away from me as she

can get. One phone call to my lawyer and I should be able to get a quick DNA test, then I can decide how best to help this kid. A greedy expression crosses her face when I jerk my wallet out of my pocket. "Fine, Jamie. I'll keep him for the night. Find a room."

She snatches the five-hundred dollars from my hand. "I'll be back first thing tomorrow," she swears, already headed to her beat up car parked in my driveway. No goodbye to the kid or even a warning she's leaving him with strangers. I have twenty-four hours to find out if the boy is really mine and figure out what the hell to do.

I can hear Evie's voice and Cody's giggle as I head toward the kitchen. Christ, things have finally calmed down between us, and now this. Evie's typical response is to overreact and run away. If she leaves this time I won't be following. She loves kids and if she assumes I abandoned him, I know she'll go. Taking a deep breath, I close my eyes, hoping for once I'm afforded the benefit of the doubt.

They're sitting at the table and a pang pierces me when familiar blue eyes glance fearfully into mine before returning to his plate. They ought to be familiar. I see in them in the mirror every damn day. Eyes my color, dark hair. Shit. What if she's telling the truth? What if I've missed years of my son's life without even realizing it? I can't even think about the life he's had with a selfish junky mother. "Hi, buddy," I say in a cheerful voice. "What are you eating?"

"Scrambled eggs," he murmurs.

"Evie is a good cook, isn't she?"

He grins at her. She's won him over already, put him at ease. "Where's my mom?"

"She had to do some stuff so you're going to hang out with us today, okay?" I half expect a tantrum, but he only nods, apparently used to being left with strangers.

Evie glances at me and runs her hand down his back. "We'll have fun."

He drains his glass of chocolate milk and spoons the last bite of egg into his mouth. Poor kid was starving. "Would you like to watch cartoons for a little while?" Evie asks, and he nods. He follows me to the living room and curls up on the couch, glued to the T.V.

Evie's arms wrap around me as soon as I step back into the kitchen, and her breath is warm on my neck as she asks, "Are you okay?"

For a second, I can't answer. I don't know how I am. An hour ago I was asleep beside my girl and everything was fine. Now I'm facing the possibility of being a father. She holds me tighter when I bury my face in her neck. "She never told you," she whispers.

"No."

"I'm so sorry."

Stepping back, I tuck her hair behind her ear. "We don't know he's mine yet."

"I know…" Her teeth are clamped on her bottom lip as she hesitates. "He looks like you."

"Yeah, I noticed. I'm going to make some calls, arrange for a DNA test. Jamie won't be back until tomorrow."

A worried expression creases her face. "What does she want? Money…or you?"

"Drugs. That's all she cares about. We were never together, love. We just fucked a couple of times. It was years ago."

"I understand. Mason, I think we should take Cody to a doctor. Who knows if he's ever had a checkup? He's so thin. And he needs clothes. She didn't leave him anything. We need to go shopping. I can get someone to cover my hours at BTC today."

"Everly, this isn't your responsibility. You don't have to be in the middle of this. I can handle it."

Her face falls. "Would you rather I go?"

"Of course not." My eyes close as I try to get a grip. "I just…shit…I don't want to scare you away again. If Cody's mine, I'll be filing for emergency custody. You need to know that."

Her smile is soft and kind as her hand squeezes mine. "I'd expect nothing less from you. He's a sweet kid, and I want to help however I can. Do you really think I'd leave you because you have a kid?"

"Maybe if you thought I'd abandoned my son," I confess.

"You'd never abandon a child. Mason, every time I've needed you, you've been there. Please let me do the same."

She gasps as I pull her back into my embrace and hug her tight. "Thank you for not thinking the worst."

"I trust you, baby, and I want to show you that you can trust me too. I love you."

"You damn well better, because I'm not letting you go."

"You need to let me go now if we're going to get anything accomplished," she says with a giggle. "I can't be glued to your chest all day."

"I have much better ways to restrain you, but it'll have to wait," I murmur in her ear, and she gives a little groan, stepping away.

"I'll go hang out with Cody until you're ready to go."

One call to my lawyer, and everything is set. We have an appointment with a clinic to get Cody checked out and get a sample of his DNA. Landon also arranges for a lab to rush the order. I'm not handing Cody back to that bitch no matter the results, but the faster we know where I stand legally, the better.

Chapter Nine

Evie

Cody is quiet in the back seat of Mason's car as we head toward the doctor's office. Mason gives me an anxious look, obviously unsure what to say to him.

"After the doctor, we'll go have some fun," I say, turning to smile at him. "Do you like to go to the movies?"

His little shoulders rise and drop. "I've never been."

"The mall has a movie theater," I tell Mason. "Maybe you two can catch a movie while I find him some clothes."

"Sounds good to me." Mason glances at Cody in the mirror. "They also have a Chuckie Cheese. We can play video games."

Cody's eyes light up. "I like video games."

He seems happier, running to join another little boy who's playing with blocks as we take a seat in the clinic's waiting room. Mason cocks an eyebrow at me. "He adapts fast. I'd have been terrified to be left with strangers at his age."

"I imagine he's used to it."

"I'm going to strangle that bitch."

"Get in line."

Cody doesn't complain as the cheerful female doctor examines him. "What's that for?" he asks when she swabs his mouth for DNA.

"We just need to check your spit." She throws us a tight

smile before leaving the room.

"Why are they checking my spit? I'm not sick. I promise."

I nod at Mason when he glances at me. He's a smart kid and he's going to hear it talked about. "They can do a test to see who your parents are, who you're related to."

"It tells them who my mom is?"

"Yeah, buddy, and your dad."

Two sets of identical blue eyes regard each other for a long minute before Cody asks, "Are you my dad?"

Mason runs a hand through Cody's hair. "I don't know, but we're going to find out, okay?"

"Okay."

They're interrupted when the doctor returns. "Is he my dad?" Cody instantly demands, and her face floods with sympathy.

"We won't know until tomorrow, honey."

Cody nods and asks, "Can I go play with the blocks?"

"That's a good idea. We're going to talk to the doctor for a minute, then we'll go," Mason says.

"Is he okay?" I ask as soon as he's left the room.

"Generally, yes, he's healthy, but there are a few issues. He's underweight and considering his history, I'm concerned he may not have been vaccinated. You need to try to locate those records if they exist."

"I'll find out," Mason assures her.

"Also, he has an advanced infestation of head lice. I can give you a shampoo, but it'll take multiple applications, and you must remove the eggs. With boys, it's sometimes easier to just shave their head. It's your decision. I'll give you a spray you need to use on any furniture, blankets, or pillows he's come into contact with."

Just the thought has me scratching my head, and the doctor laughs. "I doubt you've been infected unless you used the same comb or pillow. Head lice is common in school age children. He'll be fine. I'd like to see him back in a few weeks for a weight check and vaccinations." After signing the paperwork and paying the bill, Mason takes the paper sack containing the lice shampoo and spray.

"We shouldn't tell Cody until we get home. Bugs in his hair might freak him out," I warn.

"Freaks me out," Mason murmurs, and I laugh, taking his hand. Cody grabs my other hand and we head to the car.

Walking between them reminds me of childhood dreams best left forgotten, and I'm suddenly struck with an overwhelming sadness. For years, I wanted a family so much the yearning was a constant gnawing ache in my gut. I'd see parents walking with children, smiling and holding hands, and it tore at me. Every single birthday that someone actually remembered a cake and candles, my wish was the same. A family. People who love me. At some point I stopped wishing and accepted some people couldn't be loved.

Mason looks at me over the top of the car after making sure Cody is buckled in the back seat. "Are you okay?"

"Fine." I force a smile. "Let's go to the mall."

"Every man's favorite place," Mason replies with a grin, rolling his eyes.

"Relax, we can stop in the salon and get you a mani/pedi."

"What's that?" Cody asks.

"Where people get their fingernails and toenails painted," I reply.

"That's for girls!"

"You tell her, pal," Mason reaches back to high five Cody, who grins back at him.

Cody stares wide eyed at the large fountain just inside the mall entrance. "Can I play in the water?" he asks, and Mason chuckles.

"That's probably against the rules, but we can throw pennies in and make a wish."

"Cool!"

Mason turns and hands me his credit card. "Get him whatever you think he needs, love. We'll catch a movie, then find you, okay?"

"Have fun."

He leans to whisper in my ear. "You could start over there at the lingerie store."

"I don't think they sell anything for him."

"Then get something for me. Something lacy." His lips land softly on mine, and he grins when a small hum escapes my throat.

"Not sure they have your size, but I'll do my best," I tease, and he smacks my ass before joining Cody at the fountain.

Nearly three hours later, I'm loaded down with bags. I hope I've thought of everything. Mason and Cody approach me, Cody babbling excitedly about the movie and showing me his new toys. "We needed Legos," Mason explains, looking like a kid himself.

"And race cars, and dinos, and boats," Cody adds.

"Let's put all this stuff in the car and head to Chuckie Cheese. I don't know about you two, but I need pizza," Mason announces.

"Yes!" Cody grabs Mason's hand as we cross the parking lot and a strange look flits across Mason's face. He's already becoming attached to this sweet little boy. For the first time, I wonder if Mason's hoping for a positive DNA match.

Chuckie Cheese is the hellhole I remember. Loud, bright and stuffed with kids, mostly unsupervised. I'm happy to wait on the pizza while they run off to play. When the food comes, I find them laughing and yelling as they sit astride a motorcycle.

Cody sits in front of Mason, and I can see his amazement when Mason tilts the bike to the right, and the biker onscreen does the same. "Let's crash him!" Cody cries, and proceeds to hit everything in their path.

Mason laughs and lifts him off the bike when the game ends. Cody eats his pizza with the same enthusiasm he showed at breakfast. He doesn't argue or complain when it's time to go. The poor kid has to be exhausted. And we still have the head lice issue to address before bed.

I make up the bed in the guest room for Cody while Mason

gives him a bath. Clippers buzz to life as I'm organizing Cody's new clothes and toys. I guess he decided shaving his head was easier. My heart aches for the boy. Five years old with a mother who doesn't give two shits about him. If he's not Mason's child, chances are he'll end up in the system just like me.

After I have everything put away, I peek in the bathroom door to see how it's going. Cody is in the bath, his hair buzzed down to a quarter inch, playing with his new plastic boats. Mason kneels beside the tub and his hand sweeps through the water, making waves to toss the boats.

"It's a storm!" Cody cries with a giggle.

"All hands on deck, sailors!" Mason replies. He's almost as wet as Cody. When he turns to give me a sheepish grin, my jaw falls to my feet. His head is shaved too!

"We got navy guy haircuts!" Cody says, beaming, and I force a smile.

"You did!" I reach to rub Cody's head. "Looking good there, sailor."

Mason gets to his feet and grabs a towel. "Time to get out, buddy. It's getting late and navy guys get up early."

"Pajamas are on his bed," I tell Mason. Leaving them to it, I return to the living room to treat the furniture with the lice spray. Good thing we caught it early. I spend a few minutes tidying up before checking on Mason and Cody.

Mason is just leaving Cody's room, a finger to his lips to shush me. "He's out. Didn't take five minutes."

I follow him to his bedroom, and when he turns to grin at me, I'm struck again by how different he looks with short hair. "What do you think?" he asks as we climb into bed.

"I think it's the sweetest thing I've ever seen anyone do for a kid." My hands travel over his scalp, feeling the bristles under my palms. Hmm, maybe this isn't so bad. But oh, I'll miss that dark floppy hair.

"You don't like it," he accuses with a chuckle.

"Mason, you're gorgeous no matter what and you know it." I run my hand over his head again. "I love how it feels."

A mischievous grin cracks his face and he jerks the blanket

off of me. I'm wearing panties and a t-shirt since we can't sleep naked with a child across the hall.

"What are you doing?" I squeal as he scoots to my knees and pulls my legs apart. Placing his head just above my knee, he drags the bristles up the tender skin of my inner thigh, then down the other. Fuck, it feels amazing. "Mason," I moan.

"Like it now?" he teases, pulling up my shirt and rubbing his temple over my nipples.

"I think you need to grow a beard."

Laughing, he tugs my panties off. "You have to be quiet. Can you keep quiet?"

"Yes," I moan as his warm breath puffs between my legs.

"That's not very quiet," he teases and delivers a long slow lick that makes me whimper. "I'm going to stop every time you make a sound."

Oh fuck. His arms wrap around my thighs, pulling me to his mouth. I swear I really try not to make a sound, but when he slips his fingers inside and sucks me hard, I can't contain it anymore and the words come tumbling out. "Oh fuck, yes, right there."

With a dark chuckle, he stops everything and peeks up at me. "I let the whimpers go, but that was definitely a sound."

"Mason." I squirm as he grips my thighs tighter.

"You going to be quiet?"

"Yes, please."

"Fuck, I love it when you beg me. Tell me what you want."

"I want you to finish what you started."

"You love it, don't you? When I eat you." His eyes are dark and filled with desire. "Tell me. I want to hear you say it."

My hands rub across his rough, fuzzy head. "I love your mouth on me. Please, lick me until I come. I can't wait anymore."

Surprise and lust fight for dominance as he groans. "Grab a pillow to scream into, baby. I'm going to make you come hard."

I'm glad I take his advice because his tongue goes to goddamn town on me and I couldn't have held back the shriek that accompanied my orgasm if I was threatened with death. Before I can recover, he has his boxer briefs off and my ankles on his shoulders. "I've never been so hard in my life. This is going to be fast," he warns, sinking into me.

I'm folded nearly in half as he pounds away, so deep inside me it's a wonder I can't taste him. I can feel another orgasm stirring, and I recognize the look of concentration on Mason's face. He's close. Time for a little payback.

"Don't come. I'm almost there."

Distress creases his features and I have to bite my lip to suppress a giggle. "Shit, Evie, I can't." Yeah, not so easy is it, Caveman?

"Wait."

With a growl, he reaches between my legs and pinches my clit, catching me off guard and shoving me into another quick hard orgasm just before he shudders against me. "Cheater," I pant.

Chuckling, he pulls me into his embrace. "I give the orders when we're naked."

"You just like to boss me around."

"You like it when I do," he accuses.

Damn it, I do. I don't understand it, but hearing him tell me to bend over or not to come instantly turns me on. "I don't want to like it," I mutter.

His hands thread through my hair. "It's okay to like it. You don't take any shit during the day. Won't let anyone control you. Letting me take control takes some of the pressure off and lets you relax."

"And it makes you happy." I can see the joy on his face when I submit to him. It gives me an idea for his upcoming birthday.

"It shows me how much you trust me."

"As long as you don't bring the whips and chains into it," I tease.

"You know I could never hurt you. I just love to have you under me, begging, depending on me to bring you pleasure."

"I love it too." I snuggle up to him and rub my palm over his fuzzy head. "And I could get used to this."

"So, I'm still your tatted Adonis?"

"Am I still your stubborn spitfire?"

"Sexy stubborn spitfire." Soft lips press against mine. "Thanks for everything, Evie. I don't know what I'd have done without you today. I haven't spent a lot of time with kids."

"You were great." I rest my palm against his cheek. "Are you nervous about the DNA results?"

"Terrified. It's not that I don't want him. But…everything will change in ways I can't even predict." He looks anxious as he asks, "How are you going to feel if he's my son?"

I give him a reassuring smile. "Happy for you and him. He couldn't ask for a better father."

"You won't be upset at all?"

"Not upset." My fingers curl absently through his chest hair. "I'd be lying if I said I'm not concerned about dealing with his mother, and how she'll fit into your life." Like whether she'll get clean and they'll reunite as a family. As badly as I've always wanted a family, I can't stand in the way if there's a chance Cody can have both his parents together.

He rolls to his back, pulling me to lie on top of him. "She'll never be anything to me. There's no reason to ever be jealous of her."

I am jealous, but not for the reason he thinks. I'm jealous of any woman who can have a baby. "I'm not jealous," I insist.

"I would be. If you had another man's baby, it'd kill me. Any little Everlys are going to belong to us." At the sight of my eyes filling with tears, he adds, "Not now, love. You know…someday, maybe. I didn't mean to freak you out."

"I can't," I whisper, laying my head on his firm chest. "I can't have kids. Ever. I'm sterile. You might want to keep that in mind, Mason. Think about it before we go any further. I can't give you a family."

Strong arms wrap around me. "Oh, Evie, sweetheart, I'm so sorry. Why didn't you tell me?"

"Never seemed like the right time."

"Were you born that way?"

"No, what Frankie and Mark did, I was too little and it damaged me…left scar tissue that prevents me from conceiving."

"Fuck, baby." His hand grips my hair and he tilts my head

so I'm looking at him. "It doesn't change anything, Panda. If we want kids, we'll adopt. There are so many kids like Cody…like you and Ian."

Nodding, I lay my head back on his chest. "Let's not talk about it tonight. We have enough on our plates at the moment."

"Okay." Mason watches as I get up and get a fresh pair of panties. "Such a shame to cover up that ass," he remarks.

"Put your underwear on. We don't want to scar the poor kid if he wakes before us." I laugh and throw him a pair of boxer briefs.

"Yes, dear."

Chapter Ten

Mason

Five year old's wake at the ass crack of dawn. There's a hesitant knock on our door before a little dark head peeks through. "Can I get up now?" he asks.

"Sure, buddy. Give me a minute to get dressed and we'll have some breakfast."

"Kay." His footsteps pound down the hall to the living room and the television blares to life. A smile curls my lips as I gaze at Evie, curled up beside me. She looks so innocent asleep. I want to protect her, wrap my arms around her and keep any pain from ever reaching her again. At the same time, I want to tear her clothes off, say filthy things to her and hear the same from her lips. No one has ever satisfied me in bed the way she does. And she loves it as much as I do. Perfect. Fucking perfect.

My heart aches at the thought of her confession last night, and I'm determined to track down the men who hurt her, who stole her ability to have children. One thing at a time, though. Today, I find out if I'm a father.

As if he's reading my mind, my phone buzzes with a call from Landon. "You have the results?" I ask, without saying hello first.

"I'm waiting on an email from the lab. I should have it in the next hour. We have a few additional issues to discuss. Your place in an hour okay?"

"I'll be here."

Evie opens one eye and peeks up at me. "Everything okay?"

"Yep." She smiles when I kiss her forehead. "Lawyer will be here in an hour with the test results."

"Let's hope he shows before Jamie."

"Either way, she isn't leaving with him."

"Good. I'm going to shower. Someone dirtied me up last night."

She squeals when I smack her ass. "I like you dirty. Hurry and join us for breakfast. I'm making pancakes."

"Mmm, on my way." She rolls over and pulls the blanket over her head. Chuckling, I tickle her bare foot before leaving the room. She'll never be a morning person.

Cody grins up at me from the couch where he's watching cartoons. "Good morning. Do you like pancakes?" I ask, and his eyes widen along with his smile. "Let's go make a mess."

He giggles and follows me to the kitchen. After I throw the ingredients together, I hand Cody a big spoon to stir the batter. He looks like he's in heaven. I suppose he's not used to having much attention paid to him.

When the pancakes are sizzling on the griddle, he looks up from his glass of milk and asks, "Do I have to go with Mom today?"

"No, buddy. We're going to figure something out." I notice he didn't say "Do I have to go home?" He probably doesn't know the meaning of the word. "Where have you been staying, Cody? Do you usually stay with your mom or someone else?"

A sigh raises his chest and he looks sad. "Aunt Karen was taking care of me, but she died so we had to leave her house. I miss Aunt Karen, and Juan. He was my friend that lived next door. He went to my school."

"I'm sorry, honey. There are people I miss too."

Curiosity fills his face. "Who do you miss?"

"My mom."

"Oh, did she die too?"

"Yes, a long time ago, when I was little."

His expression turns thunderous. "I don't miss my mom. I

hate her."

I place a plate of syrup smothered pancakes in front of him. "Why do you hate her?" I'm trying to sound nonchalant. I don't want him to think I'm questioning him.

"She made me leave Juan and my school. She gets mad if I'm hungry or I don't want to sleep in the car. It's cold in the car at night, and boring."

"You're right. No one should ever have to sleep in a car. Yuck." Evie walks in, and I see the dismay in her eyes at the topic of conversation.

"Hi, Evie!" Cody greets. "We're having pancakes."

"All right! Can I eat with you?"

"Uh-huh." He scoots his stool over and pats the one beside him. Look at the little rugrat try to charm her.

"Cody was telling me how much he likes school," I tell her.

"That's great. Did you like to color?"

"Uh-huh, and I learned letters. I want to read, but I can't."

"Don't worry, you'll learn. You're very smart." Evie rubs his head.

"That's what my teacher said."

"Do you remember the name of your school?" I ask.

He grins up at me. "Yeah, Little Learners Preek-school. My teacher, Ms. Anna, said we were her best little learners."

"I'll bet you were," I reply, noting the name of the school for later. It's a good place to start looking for shot records.

His face drops at the sound of a knock on the door. "Is it my mom?"

"I'll go see. You just finish eating." I'm relieved to see Landon at the door, briefcase in hand. "Well," I demand, before he's even through the door.

"The boy is yours."

The floor shifts beneath my feet. I feel like I just got punched in the solar plexus. My lungs have decided to quit processing oxygen. Evie and Cody step into the room, and Evie takes one look at me and sends Cody to his room to get dressed. Her arms are around me, her soft voice in my ear. "Breathe, sweetheart."

"I'm okay," I gasp. How humiliating. Why don't I just swoon like a proper damsel in distress? "He's mine, Panda. Cody is my son." Tears spill down Evie's cheeks as I do my best to blink mine back.

I look up to see Cody standing uncertainly in the doorway. "Come here, buddy."

"What's wrong?" he asks. "Why is Evie crying?"

"I'm just very happy," Evie assures him.

"Oh. Why are you happy?" Evie glances at me, and I pull my son onto my lap.

"Because we just found out I'm your dad, and I wanted to be your dad so much."

His little face lights with joy. "Really? The spit test?"

Everyone laughs. "Yep. Spit tests don't lie."

"So I can stay with you?" he asks, his eyes glowing with hope. Landon gives me a quick nod. "Yes. I'm going to take care of you. Do you understand? You won't ever run out of food or sleep in a car again."

"Can I go to school?"

"When it starts in the Fall. You'll be a big Kindergarten man."

"Yay!" Hopping off my lap, he dances around the living room.

Landon nudges my shoulder. "We have a few issues to discuss, Mason. Preferably before Ms. Weldow returns."

"Let's go play outside while your dad talks with his friend a minute, okay? We can try out your wiffle ball bat," Evie suggests.

"Okay!" He bounds out the back door.

Evie bends to kiss me and whispers, "You'll be a fantastic father. Take your time. Do what you need to do."

Landon presents me with a ton of paperwork and advises me we have an emergency custody hearing this afternoon. The good news is that Jamie not only has a criminal record a mile long, but also three outstanding warrants for possession, prostitution, and so help me, armed robbery. Custody will be a cinch. "Armed robbery?" I ask, and Landon nods.

"She knocked over a convenience store with a junky pal of hers. Shoved a pistol in the man's face. You picked a real winner here, Reed."

"She wasn't like that when we met. Once the drugs got hold of her, I couldn't pull her back. How much time is she facing?"

"Once the prosecutor is presented with Cody's medical report, I expect a charge of child neglect or endangerment to be added. All together, probably ten to fifteen years."

"So, when she shows back up here?"

"Call the cops, discreetly, so she doesn't run."

I run my hands through my hair, anxiety gripping me. "I'm sure there are a million things to be done I'm not aware of. The doctor needs shot records, the school…"

Landon squeezes my shoulder. "You have time to work all that out. Right now, all you have to do is get to know your son and show up in court at three-thirty today."

I take a breath and get a grip. He's right. "Now," Landon continues, "I have some information on Mr. Perkins."

I glance over my shoulder to be sure Evie hasn't returned before we discuss her father. She wasn't real thrilled with the news he was alive and hasn't brought it up since. "You found his address?"

"I did, but if you intend to speak with him, you'd better hurry. He's dying of pancreatic cancer. He has only a few months at most."

"Shit. Okay, one thing at a time. I'll be in touch to arrange something soon. In the meantime, Evie isn't to know."

I have my brothers and now a son. Someday soon I'll make Evie my wife. So much family, something my girl will never have. Not even children with her own blood. I want to at least give her a chance to meet her father before he dies.

"I also have news on Daniel Fennel." My hands instantly ball into fists. The son of a bitch tried to kill Evie. I should have taken him out when I had the chance and spared her a trial.

"Have they set a date for the trial?"

"There won't be a trial. He plead guilty to stalking and attempted murder. Sentencing is next month. He won't be a problem for you or Ms. Hall." Relief floods through me. We can put the whole thing behind us.

Landon gathers the paperwork I've signed and shakes my hand. "I'll see you in court this afternoon."

"Thanks for everything." I owe this guy a bonus.

The custody hearing was a breeze and I now have temporary custody of my son.

Alex and Parker are standing outside the courtroom when I emerge, my brain churning with a million things I need to do.

"Asshole!" Parker barks. "Why didn't you tell us?"

Damn it all. Evie must've called them. "I haven't known for twenty-four hours myself."

"Of all the women to knock up, Jamie Weslow? Dude, if she had as many cocks sticking out of her as she's had in her, she'd look like a porcupine."

"Yeah, well, blame the condom company."

"I'm an uncle," Alex announces, and Parker grins.

"Fuck, yeah, we are. When can we meet him?"

I don't want to overwhelm Cody, but I want him to meet his family, to see he has more people who'll love him. "Come over this evening."

"Is there anything you need for him?" Alex asks.

"Evie pretty much cleaned out the mall," I reply. "But thanks."

"Mason, we're here if you need anything. A babysitter, whatever," Parker volunteers, his hand clamped on my shoulder.

I glance at my brothers, the two people I know always have my back. "I have no fucking idea what I'm doing," I confess.

"You'll learn as you go, like all parents," Alex assures me. "And we'll be here to help."

"Cody's a great kid. You'll love him."

"Of course we will," Parker replies, climbing in his truck.

"See you tonight."

Alex waves as he takes off. I'm so lucky to have them. I can't imagine a life with no family, like Evie.

Evie and Cody sit cross legged on the porch, a game board between them. "Daddy! I beat Evie at Candyland. She keeps getting stuck in the molasses swamp!" He bounds to his feet.

I barely hear the rest of his sentence. My heart is pulled tight at the word "daddy". I'm Daddy. "That's great, buddy."

Evie's soft smile speaks volumes. She recognizes the effect my new moniker has on me. "Did the judge say yes?" Cody asks, bouncing around like a sugared up bunny. "Do I get to stay?"

I sweep him up into a hug. "Yes. You're my boy. You're staying with me."

"Yay!"

"You have two uncles who can't wait to meet you. They'll be coming by after dinner."

"I have uncles." His little face screws up. "Will they like me?"

"Are you kidding? They'll love you." I run my palm over his head. "Just like I do. Are you hungry?"

"Evie's making spaghetti," he says, flashing her a charming smile. "Can I go watch cartoons?" he asks, turning back to me.

"Sure, buddy."

Evie wraps her arms around me after he runs into the house. "How are you?"

"Overwhelmed, terrified, and ecstatically happy."

"Your brothers will love him. He'll fit right in." Her hands cup my ass and squeeze.

"This is going to limit my ability to bend you over whenever I want," I growl, licking her ear.

"All part of dating a DILF."

"You did not call me that."

"I believe I did."

Alex and Parker show up loaded down with presents, and Alex carries a cake with Welcome Cody written in icing. Cody takes to my brothers instantly. "Why do I got presents? It's not Christmas."

"No, but it's a celebration," Parker says, leaning toward him. "Plus, I know where to find the best toys."

Cody giggles as he unwraps a box with four ping pong ball guns. Within seconds, the house is filled with flying ping pong balls as a war breaks out. Evie peeks out of the kitchen where she's cutting the cake and gives me an I-told-you-so wink.

It's good to see Cody having fun, coming out of his shell. I have no illusions to the struggle in his future. He's losing his mother, the only family he's ever known. No matter how much he voices his desire to stay with us, or complains about how she treats him, she's still his mother.

We're biologically programmed to love our parents and seek their acceptance, even if they're horrible people. I struggled the first few years after my mother's death, because as strong as my hatred for my father was, I also missed him.

Cody's little face is flushed as he plops on the couch to rest, and Evie brings him a juice box. Excitement widens his eyes when Alex retrieves a large box tied with a ribbon. "Here you go, pal. Some stuff for rainy days."

"Art stuff. We have art at school!" Cody cries, digging in the box. Out comes a giant box of crayons, markers, and colored pencils. Evie stacks the supplies on the coffee table as Cody exclaims over each item before moving on to the next. Glue, safety scissors, glitter—that should be fun to clean up—and thick stacks of paper, every art supply you could think of.

Cody's brow wrinkles at the cans of brightly colored Play-Doh. "Is it paint?"

Alex pops open a can of blue. "It's Play-Doh. You can make stuff with it."

Cody squishes it and grins, "Will you make something, too?"

"What should I make?" Joy emanates from Cody when Alex

sits on the floor beside him and opens the cans.

"Boats?" Cody suggests, and they set to it. It's sort of an irresistible activity, and before long we're all gathered around, sculpting.

Cody examines our attempts, complimenting Evie's flower and my shark. Parker tries to block the cock and balls model he's made from Cody's sight while flashing it at the rest of us, a silly grin on his face. I swear, he'll never grow up. He isn't quick enough, and Cody gets a peek. "What's that?"

"A rocket," Parker replies, not missing a beat.

"Oh, it looks like a wiener," he remarks in a disinterested tone, causing the room to erupt in laughter. After the Play-Doh is cleaned up and put away, I hand out slices of cake and everyone digs in. Sugaring up the kid before bed probably isn't wise, but what the hell, we're celebrating.

A knock at the door fills me with dread. No one but my brothers just drop in. It has to be Jamie. This is going to be ugly. I don't want to let her in, but I need to stall her long enough for the cops to show up.

The babbling begins the second I let her in and continues as she follows me into the house. "Sorry I'm late, but I had trouble getting a room. I just need a little more money and I'll take Cody, you…" Her prattle fades at the sight of everyone in the living room. "You having a party?" Her nails pick at the skin on her arms while her gaze brushes over Cody without acknowledging him.

"I got presents," Cody announces. "Look." A quick grin flashes across her face as she replies without looking at him.

"That's great, baby. Mason, really, I need to go, and I need some more money."

Evie picks up her phone, nodding to inform me she's calling Officer Roberts, and disappears into the kitchen. Parker scoops Cody onto his hip. "Let's get that icing off your face and you can show me your room, okay, partner?" I'm grateful he's removing him from a volatile situation.

You ever see a junky desperate for money? When she finds out she isn't getting any, rage is the likely result. I'm having trouble containing my own anger when I turn to her. "More money? For Cody, I'm sure, right? Like the five hundred I just gave you."

"It got stolen," she snaps. "And you fucking owe me anyway. You think it's cheap raising a kid?"

"You aren't fucking raising him! You bring him here starving and crawling with head lice, and you think I'm going to let you leave with him?" I swallow the insults and names I want to call her, aware Cody may be able to hear.

"If you just gave me more money, I could feed him more!"

"Bullshit! You want him for the welfare check and because you can use him to get sympathy. People see a kid, they'll give you money. So you can put it in your vein while your son goes to sleep hungry in a damn car!"

Rage takes over as she realizes I'm not giving her a damn thing. "I'm taking my kid. You can't stop me." Stalking across the room, she yells, "Cody, get your ass out here! We're leaving!" She bares her teeth at me like a wild animal when I grab her arm. "Don't touch me! I'll call the cops!"

"Do that," I scoff, relocating her ass to the chair.

"Mom?" Cody's voice is small. He stands in the hallway, clinging to Parker's hand. He has wiped the icing from his face and put on his new Hulk pajamas. Evie returns and lingers quietly beside Alex.

"Get your shoes," Jamie snaps at Cody. "We're leaving."

"I don't wanna."

"Get your goddamn shoes!"

He flinches but shakes his head. "I'm staying with Daddy."

"He's not your daddy you worthless little shit."

Cody buries his face in Parker's neck as he picks him up and takes him back to the bedroom. His timing is good because the crack of Evie's palm on Jamie's cheek rings out a few seconds later. "Don't you ever call a child worthless, you pathetic excuse for a human being," Evie hisses. Alex steps in front of Evie, and I shove Jamie back into the chair when she lunges at her.

"He isn't even yours, you stupid son of a bitch!" Jamie screams.

"I have a DNA test that says he is. And I was granted

custody just a few hours ago, so save your foul breath. I feel sorry for your future cellmate." It thrills me to be the one to tell her she's busted. "Once the judge realized you have three outstanding warrants, custody was no longer an issue."

Fear fills her face when there's another knock at the door. "And there's your ride," I taunt. Evie leads the officers into the living room.

"Jamie Weslow?" Officer Roberts asks. When she fails to respond, he produces a set of handcuffs and rattles off her rights.

"You can't do this! She…she hit me!" Jamie nods at Evie while the officer cuffs her. "I want to press charges!"

"I see no evidence of that," Roberts replies, ignoring the red handprint glowing on her cheek.

"Thank you." I shake hands with him and his partner.

"Just worry about your boy," Roberts advises. "We've got this. She'll be in Judge Hennon's courtroom." Judge Hennon works with Striking Back and will have no problem holding a neglectful mother and armed robber without bail. Threats and curses spew from her lips all the way to the squad car. I don't envy the officers' ride back with her. The silence after they're gone is a relief.

"I'm sorry," Evie says softly. "I shouldn't have lost it. When she called him worthless, I…"

My lips on hers put an end to her apology, and she squeezes me tight when I embrace her. "You were perfect."

Alex agrees. "I wanted to beat the shit out of her too, Ev. No worries. She deserves way more than she got."

"I have to talk to Cody. I'm sure he's upset." What the hell am I supposed to say to him? What do I say to a boy who knows his mother doesn't give a shit?

"Go ahead," Alex encourages. "We'll clean up."

♡

Cody sits on Parker's lap on the bed. Parker glances up at

me and continues reassuring him as I take a seat beside them. "Bad drugs make people really sick. It makes them say and do bad things. It's not because there's anything wrong with you. Your mom is sick. She's going to a place where they'll help her get better."

"So she won't take bad drugs?"

"That's right." Parker rubs his back.

Cody looks up at me, and the fear in his eyes breaks my heart. "What if she comes back?"

"She can't come back, buddy."

"Cause the cops took her to jail?"

Shit. I was hoping he didn't hear that. "Yes, she did bad things and has to stay in jail, but they'll help her get better."

His mouth turns down as he crawls off Parker's lap and lays his head on his pillow. "So, I'll never see her again?"

"We can visit if you want to."

Indecision is reflected on his face. "I don't want her to yell or hit me."

"That isn't going to happen. No one is going to hurt you. I promise." I pull the covers over him. "Everyone gets angry. You just have to find a good way to let it out. Yelling and hurting people is wrong."

Yawning, he asks, "How do you let it out?"

Parker grins and slaps my leg. "You should bring him to the gym tomorrow."

"I like to kick and punch a big punching bag. Would you like to try that?"

His eyes light up. "Like a boxer? Are you a boxer?"

Parker leans over like he's sharing a secret. "Your dad is a champion fighter."

"Really? Do you slam guys like John Cena?"

"Not exactly." I laugh and kiss his forehead. "I'll take you to the gym tomorrow and show you."

"Okay." The poor kid is exhausted after the night he's had and his eyes drift shut.

Parker pulls me into a one armed hug as we leave the room. "He'll be fine."

Chapter Eleven

Evie

"Will you please tell me where we're going?" I ask as Mason steers the car into a middle class neighborhood. "There's someone you need to meet." We park in front of a small brick house and I'm led to the door. Standing on the porch, Mason takes my hands in his. "You've been so wonderful to Cody and helped me so much with him. I have every intention of making you part of my family as soon as you're ready, but I know that doesn't fill the hole left by your own family. You should know someone with your blood."

"Mason, there's no one…"

My statement is cut short when Mason opens the door and leads me into the living room. A man sits on the couch. He's obviously very sick, his hanging skin betraying a recent weight loss. He's wrinkled, bald, and hunched over, but I'd recognize his eyes anywhere. Eyes I last saw being swallowed by murky water.

"Everly?" he asks, his voice raspy. "God, you grew up beautiful."

No. No, he didn't do this. Didn't spring my father—the father I thought was dead—on me without warning. I can't do this. "Evie!" I hear Mason call as I flee down the stairs. His arms wrap around my waist, preventing my escape. "Evie, stop! It's okay, sweetheart."

"I need to get out of here. Now." Water. Darkness. Blood. My father's eyes. The world spins and I shove him off me just in time as my lunch makes a reappearance.

"I got you, baby." He holds my hair back until I'm done and hands me a water bottle from the car. "I'm sorry. I didn't think meeting your father would upset you like this."

"You knew I wouldn't come," I choke. "That's why you tricked me." I jerk away when he tries to hug me, and his shoulders droop.

"It wasn't a trick. I just didn't want you to worry or obsess over it. I thought it'd be easier for you."

A sickening thumping in my head makes it hard to think, and I massage my temples. "What can I do, Panda? What do you need?"

"Take me home."

"Okay." He opens my car door and makes a quick call. "Yeah, can you take Mr. Perkins home, please? No, it didn't go well. Shut the fuck up, Devon." The phone is tossed onto the seat.

When I note the direction he's driving, I shake my head. "Home, Mason. Take me to my apartment."

"Evie, don't. I'm sorry. I didn't mean to…"

"I know, but I need to be alone. I can't deal with this and act happy with Cody, and…" I babble, hearing the panic in my own voice.

"You promised not to run."

"I'm not. I'm not leaving you."

"I already arranged for Cody to spend the night with Parker. I figured we'd need some time alone. There's no reason for you to stay at your apartment."

"Fine," I sigh, swiping at the tear running down my cheek.

When we enter Mason's house, Alex is sitting on the couch. He gives Mason a questioning look and looks at me with sympathy when Mason shakes his head. So I guess everyone knew what was going on but me. "You okay, Ev?" he asks.

"Fantastic," I reply, kicking off my shoes.

"Is there anything I can do?"

"Ask Mason. Apparently, he makes all my decisions," I

reply, making a beeline for the back patio and flopping onto a lounger.

I know I'm being a bitch when Alex isn't to blame for any of this, but now that the shock is wearing off, anger is taking its place. He just decided I was going to meet my father, then made it happen with no thought of how I might feel about it.

When he first told me my father was alive, I was shocked. I really didn't want to deal with it or think about it, so I didn't. I just pretended I never heard it. I accepted the death of my parents a long time ago.

There has been plenty of other drama to keep me distracted. Since I met Mason I've been knocked out, almost drowned, fell in love, agreed to move in with him, discovered he has a son, and come face to face with my dead father. No wonder I feel like a psycho.

A few minutes pass before I hear Mason's back door slide open. I swear if he comes near me, I'm shoving his ass in the pool. It's Alex that takes a seat beside me and asks, "Plotting his violent death?"

"Violent maiming, perhaps."

His arm slides around my shoulders. "I tried to tell him it was a bad idea. So did Parker, but he was adamant."

"Why?" I groan. "Why was it so fucking important I meet my dad that he'd corner me like that?"

"He's got his own daddy issues, Ev. Especially with our father's execution date approaching. I think he wanted to reunite you with your father because he's losing his."

I look up to see a dismayed look on Alex's handsome face. "What execution?"

His eyes widen and he shakes his head. "He didn't tell you."

"He said your dad is on death row, but I know people stay there for years with appeals and stuff."

"Appeals are up. He's got six months at most. He keeps calling, wanting us to visit, but Mason and Parker won't hear it."

I pull Alex into a warm hug. "I'm sorry. I had no idea. How are you handling it?"

"Still deciding whether to talk to him. Mason doesn't care,

but Parker would be really pissed."

"Well, decide for yourself. If you want to visit, then do it."

Alex grins. "Mason told me you're moving in together. I'm happy for you."

"It doesn't seem like a solid idea at the moment," I admit.

"So, you're pissed at him. I'm sure it won't be the last time. Argue, kick his ass, and move on. He loves you so much, Ev, he's just an idiot."

Mason arrives just in time to hear my snort of laughter. "Why do I feel like I'm being talked about?"

"Not a total idiot," I murmur, and Alex laughs. "Thanks for the talk," I add, kissing him on the cheek.

"Anytime, honey." Alex punches Mason in the arm and heads home.

Mason sits beside me, our placemat of promises in hand. "You have something you want to say?" I demand.

"I thought you might want to re-read the part about not running and talking about our problems."

"I didn't run."

"You were going to."

"Maybe we should add I promise not to trick my girlfriend into confronting dead relatives."

"Seems awfully specific," he replies, and I can't help cracking a grin at his crooked smile. Damn him.

"You should pay more attention to the honesty and no secrets part."

"Touché."

"He's dying, isn't he? My father?"

"Yes, he has a couple of months if he's lucky. I just didn't want you to regret not talking to him before he dies."

I stare intently into his eyes. "Like you'll regret not talking to your father? Alex told me about the execution."

"That's different."

"Bullshit. How would you like it if I blindfolded you and led you to the prison for a surprise visit?"

His posture shows his stress, his fingers sweeping over his scalp while he bends over, leaning his elbows on his knees. Staring at the floor, he replies, "You're right. I didn't see it that way. I shouldn't have went about it the way I did."

"You can't make my decisions for me. I make my own choices."

I'm wrapped tight in his embrace. "I'm sorry. Can you forgive me?"

My arms tighten around him and I bury my face in his neck. "Yes, I'm sorry I freaked out."

"Just run to me, baby, not from me."

"I'm still mad at you," I murmur, and he gives me a cocky grin.

"You can take it out on me in bed."

I smack his chest. "You're awful!"

"But you love me." His kiss is tender and sweet.

"So much," I sigh.

Chapter Twelve

Mason

Today is my birthday and judging by the mischievous smile on Evie's face when Alex mentions it, she has something up her sleeve. "I'll bring Cody back tomorrow evening," Alex tells her with a wink.

"What's she up to?" I ask Alex when she leaves the room.

"I'm not ruining her surprise. You'll see."

"Asshole."

"Dipshit."

Evie vibrates with nervous excitement as we pull onto the interstate. What the hell is she up to? All she would tell me was to pack an overnight bag. I swear if she's rented a room at one of those bed and breakfast places women always like, I'll kill Alex for not telling me. Then I'll run every other guest away by fucking her until she screams the house down. That's all I really want for my birthday. Unfettered access to her naked sexy body.

I'm stunned when she parks the car outside a Fantasy Inn. It's like she read my mind. I've seen advertisements for these hotels. Each room is decorated and equipped to play out a specific sexual fantasy. The brochure I read showed rooms set up like a doctor's office, a jungle, a spaceship, even an old western saloon. "You fulfilling a fantasy, love?" I ask.

"One of yours. Come on." Holy shit. What has she got

planned? I'm lead through an opulent lobby and into an elevator. Evie grins up at me, nearly shaking with excitement. We exit on the fifth floor and she hesitates outside the suite door.

Brandishing the key card and a mischievous smile that makes me want to remove her panties with my teeth, she says, "I hope you're ready for a long naked night."

"Open the door before I take you up against it," I growl, and she giggles. I'm completely floored when we step into a BDSM themed room. Painted a dark gray with deep red furniture, it manages to look intimidating and sexy at the same time. A rack of spanking implements line one wall. Paddles, floggers, riding crops...you name it. Just below the rack is a padded bench, complete with restraints. As I look around the suite, I realize every piece of furniture has carabiners and swivels attached in multiple places to hold restraints.

"Speechless," Evie remarks. "I never thought I'd see the day." Her voice trembles a bit when I turn to gaze at her. "They have a dungeon room, but it seemed like a bit much. This one is sort of BDSM light." Her shy grin makes her look so young and innocent. "I'm yours to command for the night."

Fuck. Me. Every inch of me wants to grab her, strip her naked and wipe the innocent look from her face. Make her scream my name until it's all she can ever think about. Instead, I slide one arm around her waist and tilt her chin up so I can stare into those gorgeous eyes. "Why do you want to do this?"

"You like to control me when I'm naked, remember?" A small embarrassed smile graces her lips. "I like it, too."

"This is an amazing surprise, sweetheart."

"You're happy?"

"You always make me happy. Now, let's talk about the rules," I tell her, hardening my voice.

"I'm not calling you Master or Sir," she warns, and I squeeze her ass.

"Any other conditions?"

"No." Her hands fall to my waist. "I trust you not to hurt me."

"Never, baby. All you ever have to do is tell me to stop."

"I'm not good at following the rules," she says, stepping back with a teasing smile. "What happens if I break one?"

"Then I'll have to correct you and teach you to behave."

"Ooh, a spanking?" Giggling, she moves quickly, dodging me as I pursue her.

"Test me and find out, love. There are only two rules. One, do what I say without arguing." Something tells me that's the one she'll have the most trouble with. "Two, you aren't allowed to wear clothes until we leave this room."

She stops and stares at me, her jaw on the floor. "I'm not staying naked!"

I grab her hips and pull her against me, grinding my hard on into her ass as I murmur in her ear. "You're going to do what I tell you to do. Now, take off your clothes and wait for me on the sofa."

Defiance flashes in her eyes, and I have to swallow a chuckle. There's not an inch of my girl that's submissive. It makes what she's doing for me mean so much more. She's going to struggle to obey, and I'm going to have the time of my life correcting her. I walk away to build a fire in the small fireplace and bump up the thermostat a few degrees so she won't be cold. I'm going to love seeing her naked all night, watching the blush spread from her chest to her neck and cheeks when I gaze at her.

When I return, she's wearing a pair of lace boyshort panties, her arms folded across her bare breasts. Here we go. I yank her panties off and smack her bare ass. "I said naked. Now, come with me."

Her eyes widen when I open a cabinet on the wall. It's full of every sex toy you could imagine, still sealed in their packages. "A sex toy mini bar?" she says with a giggle.

"Oh, Evie, we are going to have so much fun." I choose a couple of packages and motion to the sofa. "Go pick a movie."

"You want to watch a movie?" she asks, stunned. No, I want to fuck her into next week, but I'm going to make her wait. I'm going to drive her crazy.

"Yep, let's relax. Would you like a glass of wine?"

"Sure, thanks." I hand her the glass, and we cuddle up on

the sofa as the movie begins. I couldn't even tell you the name of it with her sitting beside me with those hard nipples, waiting for me to touch her. She keeps peeking at me, and finally slides a hand up my thigh. "Take your clothes off."

"Are you giving me orders?"

"No," she sighs.

"Are you cold?"

"No, but you could make me sweaty." Her hand closes over the bulge in my jeans, and I have to picture every hard on killing image I can manage. Rotten meat. Crying babies. Old wrinkled balls. Yeah, that'll do it.

"No, you'll wait." I grin at her stubborn expression. "Do we need to review the rules?"

"Are you trying to torture me?"

"When I'm torturing you, you'll know it, sweetheart."

"Fine," she grumbles, curling up beside me again. As we watch the movie, I trail a finger up and down her thigh, noting how her breathing stutters. I want her desperate, begging for my cock. She squirms and shifts, trying to get my hand between her legs. Instead, I throw my arm around her shoulder, and she groans.

A few seconds later, she has a new plan. Sitting back on the couch with her knees bent, she gives me a sideways glance before running a finger between her legs. For a second, I'm mesmerized by the way her head falls back, her soft brown waves spreading over her bare shoulders, her lips parting as she pleasures herself. Shit, I have to get a grip.

"No touching yourself," I order pulling her hand away.

"Damn it, Mason! I want to come."

"You'll come when I tell you to. Who's in charge?" A moan rattles her chest as I pinch her nipple and slide my hand between her legs. Christ, she's soaked.

"You are."

"Then behave," I order, sitting back and removing my hand.

"Stop torturing me."

"Okay, sweetheart, you want torture, you got it." Grabbing

her hand, I lead her to a padded wall where leather cuffs are attached. She doesn't even try to fight me when I secure her arms and spread her legs before restraining them as well. She wants me to touch her.

Her skin blooms pink as I stare at her, my gaze climbing and falling over the naked goddess in front of me. Her tongue dives eagerly into my mouth when I kiss her, letting only our mouths touch. "I told you to get naked."

"Uh-huh," she moans, kissing me again.

"You didn't obey. So you'll wait." The look I get when I step away from her would set a house on fire.

"Mason! Goddamn it!" She continues to hurl obscenities while I saunter over to the toys and open the packages.

"Flattery will get you nowhere, Panda," I call.

Her eyes land on the two toys in my hand when I return and she asks, "What are you going to do?"

"Does it ache, love? Are you aching for my cock?"

"Yes, please."

"It's going to get worse before it gets better," I growl, dropping to my knees and licking inside her. Squeals fill the room as she pulls on the restraints.

"Oh fuck! Mason! Yes!"

I replace my mouth with my fingers. "Have you ever used a vibrator, Evie?" I ask, rubbing her spot while she thrusts into my hand.

"Yes," she groans. "They're too intense. Make me come too fast. Too strong."

"We'll see about that."

"No," she moans as I withdraw my fingers and pick up a g-spot vibrator and a tiny one that clips to my fingertip. She'll be through the ceiling. I gently slip the g-spot vibe into her, working her spot without turning on the vibration. "Oh god, Mason, so good, don't stop." Her head falls back, and I swear I've never seen anything so fucking erotic. Her lips are open, her wrists drawn tight against the restraints, her entire body flushed and sweaty.

"You don't have permission to come," I remind her, and she groans in frustration. When I flip on the vibe, her hips thrust forward and she shrieks.

"It's too much! I can't stand it!"

"Yes, you can. I'm not done with you." I turn on the fingertip vibe and brush over her clit. The result is fantastic. A tremor runs through her entire body and she screams my name as she comes and comes. Keeping the fingertip vibe on her, I remove the g-spot vibe and kneel in front of her.

"No more," she pleads.

"You came before I told you to. Now, I want another one."

"I can't!"

"I know you can, baby."

Writhing and cursing, my name falls from her lips again and again as I stroke her with the fingertip vibe. "Please, Mason," she moans.

I press the vibe against her clit and hold it there and she goes wild, bucking and fighting the restraints until her cries fill the room again. "Are you going to obey?" I ask.

"Yes," she whispers, and I relent, tossing the toy aside and untying her arms and legs. She falls into my arms, panting and coated in sweat.

"Did I hurt you?" I brush her hair from her forehead.

"No, but don't let go. I've never come that hard."

"I'll never let go." Sweeping her up in my arms, I carry her to the bed. "My turn now, love. Bend over the bed." She obeys, and I grab one of the ties attached to the bedpost. In a few seconds she's bent over the bed, her sexy ass in the air, hands stretched in front of her, trussed up and helpless.

"I'm going to fuck you hard and fast Evie," I warn, shoving my pants and underwear down.

"Oh god." I know she loves it when I talk dirty to her. When I sink into her, my control disintegrates. My eyes are fixed on her bouncing ass as I drive into her again and again. She's so fucking tight and hot. My world narrows. All that exists is this woman, panting and crying out as I work her hard.

She clenches around me as another orgasm seizes her, and it sends me over the edge. When my head clears, I run my hand down her sweaty back, planting a kiss on her right cheek. "Are you okay?"

"No, you fucked me to death. My vagina is dead. Call a coroner."

Chuckling, I pull out and step back to admire her, tied and bent over the bed. "Do you have any idea how beautiful you are? I'm going to remember this the rest of my life, baby."

"Mmm, good. Now untie me."

"You giving orders again?" I run a finger between her cheeks, and she stiffens.

"No," she whimpers. She's so afraid of anything anal, and I really want to show her how good it can feel.

"Relax, my girl. I just want to touch you. I won't hurt you."

Gasping, she pulls on the restraints when I spread her natural lube up and over her little hole. "How's that feel?" I murmur, rubbing small circles without penetrating her. Fire races across her cheeks. She likes it, but she's embarrassed. "Answer me, Evie."

"Good," she whispers, pressing her face into the bed.

When she relaxes again, I press the tip of my finger inside her, and she moans. Working it gently in and out, a little deeper each time, I murmur, "That feels even better, doesn't it?"

"Yes, but I don't think I can come again. I'm done in."

Sliding my finger out, I reply, "I just wanted to show you there's nothing to fear."

She shakes the feeling back into her hands when I untie her and grins up at me. "What now?"

"Now you let me take care of you. Let's have a bath."

Evie sits between my legs and leans back against my chest as I draw the wet cloth across her skin. "Mmm, feels like my birthday," she remarks with a soft smile.

"You like being my love slave." It amuses me that she's so independent, so hard headed, yet in the bedroom gets turned on by being dominated. She hates that she loves it, and I can't resist teasing her.

"I love being with you."

"Same here, love." I caress her soft wet skin, and we spend long minutes just enjoying each other with only the sounds of our breathing and the lapping of the water breaking the silence.

"Sweetheart?"

"Hmm?"

"Have you given any more thought to speaking with your father?"

Her shoulders rise and fall on a deep sigh. "He gave me away, let me think he was dead."

"I know," I reply, despising the sound of hurt in her voice. "Are you going to talk to your father?"

"No."

"But you think I should? No hypocrisy there."

"Your father didn't murder anyone, Evie."

Her fingers thread through mine. "You don't know that. You said he was in the mob. He probably killed people."

She's got a point. "Did he ever hurt you?"

"No, not that I remember, but he threw me away. Why should I give a shit that he wants to see me now?"

I shift her to sit on my thigh so I can see her face. "You don't do it for him. You do it for you. To ask questions and get closure."

"And you don't need that?"

"I was there when he killed her. I don't have anything to say to him. There's nothing he can say."

Nodding, she lays her head on my shoulder. "I understand. You can talk to me about it anytime, Mason, you know that? I can just listen."

"I know, sweet girl."

Grinning up at me, she changes the subject. "I'm starving. Are you going to feed me before you defile me again?"

"There's a steakhouse across the street," I suggest.

"I'll have to get dressed. You'll need to put your alpha tendencies on hold."

"I don't know. There's a brand new butt plug in there you could wear," I taunt, knowing full well she'd never go for it.

"Ha!" Water runs down her plump little ass when she stands to step out of the tub, and I can't resist a squeeze.

"Vibrating panties?" I call after her as she heads for the bedroom, wrapped in a towel.

"Never going to happen, Reed!"

I'm going to marry this woman.

It was, hands down, the best birthday of my life. After dinner we experimented with some of the other instruments. I wish I had a picture of her bent over and strapped to the spanking bench, her upturned ass round and pink.

We play with the thin paddle and a flogger, both lightweight and not too painful. I could never hurt her or make her cry, but watching her squirm around, not knowing whether I'm going to spank or pleasure her damn near makes me come in my pants. Spank bank material for the rest of my life.

All the kinky stuff gets tossed aside and I make love to her slowly before bed, trying to show her how much I love what she's done for me. How much I love her. She wraps her warm little body around mine as we drift off to sleep.

When I wake to the sight of her sprawled out on top of the covers, naked and inviting, I know just how to start the day. Still deeply asleep, she barely moves when I spread her legs wide and cuff her ankles. Worried she might be afraid if she wakes unable to move, I leave her hands free.

She arches her hips at the first swipe of my tongue, responding to me even while she sleeps. Her eyes don't stay closed for long, and a low moan fills the room. "Well, good morning," she says, her voice sleep husky and sexy.

"Don't mind me. I haven't had breakfast yet."

"It is the most important meal of the day," she murmurs, grabbing my ears and pulling me against her.

I can make her come almost instantly this way, but I draw it out, bringing her close a few times until she starts cursing. "Fuck...Mason."

"I can do this all day, love."

"You want me to beg? Please, please make me come."

"I want you to marry me," I blurt.

She freezes and stares down at me in shock. "What?"

"You heard me." I nibble on her, right where I know she's most sensitive.

"Mason!" Her hands clutch my ears and jerk my head up.

"You did not just propose while going down on me."

I didn't plan to, but that doesn't mean I'm not serious. "I'll do it again however you want me to. As many times as I need to ask." I end the discussion by planting my face back between her legs, eating her ravenously until she screams my name, pulsing under my tongue.

She's quiet as we gather our things and leave the hotel. As we near home, she turns to me. "I need to think about it. I love you…I just…it's so fast."

"You're mine, Evie, forever. You know it as well as I do. I'll be right here waiting when you accept it."

A few days after my birthday, Evie asks me to accompany her to meet her dad. "He's in a hospice. They don't expect him to live much longer," she explains. "I'm going against my better judgement." Sweet brown eyes meet mine. "I don't want to go alone."

"I'll be right beside you, love," I reply, kissing her temple.

The hospice is just outside the city. Surrounded by flower gardens, it sits beside a small pond. A walking path wide enough for a wheelchair to traverse winds around the building, dotted with benches and rest areas. Some of the more ambulatory patients are sitting with family or wandering along the path.

William Perkins is in no shape to be outdoors. Evie's hand tightens in mine when she approaches the emaciated man tucked into a hospital bed. "I've got you, Panda," I murmur, sitting beside her on the small sofa adjacent to the bed.

"Everly, it's so good to see you." William's voice is weak, but steady. "You look like your mother, your beautiful mother."

"Thank you," Evie replies, shifting in her seat.

"I'm so glad you came. I know I don't deserve it, but I wanted a chance to explain."

Evie nods, her hands twisting in her lap. "I need that. There are things I need to know."

"I didn't want things to be this way."

"Why did you leave me?" Evie demands.

"To keep you alive. I was in deep with some bad men. I admit, I've done some shit in my time, sold drugs, weapons." Coughing, he winces before continuing. "But I never hurt anyone."

"I was working for the Rivera brothers one night, and we were going to a customer's house to collect. He was in debt to the brothers up to his eyeballs. The plan was to scare him and take whatever he had of value. At least that's what they told me.

"The man couldn't pay, and they beat him nearly to death. When they were done with him, one brother went upstairs, and I heard a gunshot. He said he shot at the safe, and I had no reason not to believe him."

Shame and regret flood his withered face. "Until I saw the news the next day reporting the death of the man and his eight month pregnant wife."

"No," Evie whispers.

"I couldn't live with it. I hadn't done it, but I was there, complicit. I went to the cops and told them everything. Promised I'd testify if they'd keep you and your mother safe. I picked you up and we were on our way to meet with an FBI agent when they found us. I tried to outrun them, but they rammed the car and flipped us into the reservoir."

Thin skinned hands scrub the tears from his eyes. "Your mother didn't make it. When they told me you survived, I'd never been so relieved and terrified. I knew the brothers would try again.

"The marshals came to the hospital and convinced me the best way to keep you safe was to give you up. Since you were young, they wouldn't have a problem finding a good family to adopt you. It was the hardest decision I've ever made. I loved you, Everly, I love you, but I would do it again if given the choice. The alternative would've given you a life of paranoia and fear. Moving constantly and changing schools. I didn't want that for you. The marshals fed the networks a fake news story announcing our deaths, changed your last name and put you in the foster care system."

"Did you know they told me you were dead?" Evie demands.

"Yes, when I went into witness protection, the whole world had to think I was dead. I thought you'd be better off without me. You'd grow up with a normal family who loves you and have a happy life." His frail hand grabs hers. "Did you? Were you happy?"

Indecision clouds her face, her desire to shock him with exactly how much hell he left her in darkening her eyes. She allows his hand to stay on hers as she replies, "I'm happy. I have good friends and a man who loves me."

"Were your new parents good to you?"

Here, she decides to tell the truth. "I never had parents. I bounced from foster home to foster home until I was ten. Then I went into a group home until I aged out."

"Fuck. Everly, I'm sorry. I know that isn't enough, but…"

"The money," Evie interrupts. "How did you get it? Am I living on blood money?"

"No. I told you, I never hurt anyone. Look." He sighs and rests his arm back on the bed. "Not all of it was earned legally. I ran a gambling ring for years and dabbled in other low brow activities. Most of it couldn't be traced back to me which is why the marshals had to let me keep it. I told them to transfer it to you on your eighteenth birthday." He gives her a soft smile. "From what I hear, you do a lot of good with it."

"Doesn't make it right," Evie grumbles.

"I guarantee you do more good with it than the cops would."

Nodding, Evie asks softly, "Did you remarry? Have more kids? Do I have any siblings?"

"No. No one could ever compete with your mother in my heart," he replies, and a monitor starts beeping beside his bed. His face has paled since we arrived.

A nurse rushes in and puts something in his IV. "I'm sorry to cut your visit short, but he needs to rest," she advises.

Quicker than I thought him capable of, William snatches

Evie's hand. "Can you forgive me? For your mother's death, for leaving you?" The desperation in his eyes puts tears in Evie's.

"Yes, I forgive you. I understand." She gives him a tentative hug before promising to return.

Silence weighs us down on the ride home. It tears me up watching Evie struggle with her emotions, trying to tell herself she doesn't care. I wish there was something I could do to make it easier for her. I'm awed by this woman. After all he put her through, she couldn't hurt him with the truth of her childhood abuse.

"When is Parker bringing Cody home?" she asks dully, curling up on the couch.

"Not until late. He took him to the drive-in theater."

"Do you just want to order-in your dinner tonight? I'm not hungry."

Her whole body sags when I wrap her in my arms. "I know it's hard, love. I'm so damn proud of you."

"For not losing it?" she scoffs.

"For being a better person than I'll ever be. Why didn't you tell him the truth of what happened to you?"

"I wanted to," she replies with a bitter laugh, and I kiss away the tear running down her cheek. "I planned on it, but the man I want to scream at doesn't exist anymore. There's an old dying man wearing his eyes."

"Do you want to go back?"

"I don't know. I think we said what we needed to say. I just want to put it all behind me. Be happy without all the drama."

"Sounds good sweetheart."

Chapter Thirteen

Evie

Ian meets me for lunch at his favorite fast food chicken place. We haven't seen much of one another lately. I don't want to be one of those girls who ignores her friends because she's dating a new guy.

"So, fill me in," he says, flopping into the booth across from me. "What have you been doing? Besides Mason."

I toss a greasy French fry at him. "It's been a long week. I met my father."

Ian chokes on his drink. "You did?"

"Mason tracked him down. He's dying of cancer and it was sort of now or never."

"How did it go?"

"Okay, I guess. We only stayed a few minutes. He said what you'd expect anyone to say on his deathbed. 'I love you, I'm sorry' et cetera."

Ian grabs my hand as I wave it about. "Stop. Drop the bullshit. You met the father who gave you away, the father you thought was dead. Quit making light of it and tell me how you're doing."

I never could put shit past him. "I feel guilty that I don't feel enough. I didn't feel a connection to him, and I should, shouldn't I? My father was a big, strong guy. This frail old man is a stranger to me. I'm sorry he's dying, but it doesn't hurt like it should." I take a bite to cover my embarrassment.

"There's no right way to feel in your situation. I'm glad you had a chance to say good-bye, Ev. You might not feel much now, but someday you'll be happy you did."

I look into my best friend's dark eyes. "Have you ever looked for your parents?" At least I've always had an idea where I came from. All Ian knows is his mother surrendered him when he was four.

Pain flashes across his features, followed by anger. "No. I don't remember them. They didn't want me. Why would I want to meet them?"

"For the same reason I did. To learn the truth, cure the curiosity."

"I'm not curious. I don't care." His stubborn expression tells me it's time to change the subject.

"Sounds familiar," I reply, grinning at him.

"Maybe we were separated at birth. You could be my sister," he teases.

"I couldn't love you more if we were."

"Same here, Ev."

"Okay, enough feelings. Tell me what you've been up to."

Blowing his raven hair out of his eyes, he grins. "I have a date this weekend. Laura's her name. She's hot as hell, and fun too. Fantastic in bed."

"Two points for knowing her name," I taunt, and he shakes his head at me. "She must be smoking if she earned a repeat performance." Ian isn't known for sticking with one girl long. Like past the morning after.

"For your information, this will be our third date, smartass."

"Yeah? If she makes it past this one, I want to meet her," I tell him.

I'm gifted with the little half smile that drives the women crazy. "You need to make sure she's good enough for me?"

"Isn't that what you did when you crashed my date with Mason?"

Feigning innocence, he sits back. "I didn't crash your date. You hadn't left yet. And yes, I had to make sure he deserves you."

"And the verdict?"

"You're perfect for each other."

It's on the tip of my tongue to tell him about Mason's proposal—minus how he did it—when my phone rings with Alex's number. "Hi, Alex, everything okay?"

"Evie, where are you?" His voice is wrong, high and fearful.

"Having lunch with Ian. What's wrong? Are you okay?" A million scenarios run through my head, none as bad as the actual explanation.

"You need to get to Community Hospital now. Mason's been shot."

If I never have to set foot in this hospital again, I'll die happy. The trip here was a blur. I know Ian was talking to me, trying to comfort me, but all I could hear was the beat of Mason's name in my ears. The harried looking lady at the desk looks at us with little interest.

"Mason Reed," I gasp. "He was brought by ambulance. How is he? Where is he?"

"Are you family?"

"What the fuck difference does that make?" I snap. "Tell me if he's alive."

"Ev," Ian warns, giving the lady a charming smile. "She's his wife," he lies. "We just got a call saying he's been shot."

The woman types the information into her computer. "He's in surgery. You can go to the waiting room on the third floor. A doctor will be with you shortly to advise you of his condition."

Alex runs down the hall toward us as soon as we step out of the elevator. We embrace each other and he says, "He's alive, in surgery, that's all they'll tell us."

"What happened?" Ian asks as we're lead to a small waiting

room where Parker leans against the wall, a fierce expression on his face.

"Officer Roberts called him to help on a domestic. The guy came back as Mason was leaving with the woman and child. Before anyone saw the gun, he shot him…twice. Roberts fired back and killed him. Called an ambulance, then called me."

Fear settles deep within me and I barely recognize my own voice. "Shot him where?"

"In the chest and stomach."

My legs fail me and I drop into a chair. "No, no, this can't happen to him."

Parker turns and slams his fist into the wall before stalking out. "Let him go," Alex advises. "He'll be back."

"Reed family?" A tall man covered in scrubs enters the room.

"Yes," Alex replies as we both jump to our feet.

"I'm Doctor March. Mr. Reed has sustained two gunshot wounds. Fortunately, they missed his heart and other vital organs, but he has suffered massive blood loss. We had to remove his spleen to stop the bleeding, but we now have it under control."

"Will he live?" I interrupt.

"He's very weak and we've had to restart his heart twice. The next few hours are crucial."

Oh god. He's saying he may not make it. That he could die. "Can we see him?" Alex asks, wrapping his arm around my shoulders.

"He'll be moved to intensive care when he's out of recovery. The nurse will let you know."

"Thank you," I whisper. Alex runs off to find Parker and tell him the news.

Ian wraps me in a hug, and I take comfort in the familiarity of his arms. "He's alive, Pup, and he's one strong son of a bitch. He'll make it."

"I need to tell him yes," I sob.

"Yes?"

"He asked me to marry him, and I said I had to think about it. Why did I do that? He has to be okay. I have to tell him yes."

"You will. You'll talk to him again." He steps back and sweeps my hair off my face. "And I want photographic evidence of you in a wedding dress," he adds with a teasing grin.

"You'll have to wear a suit."

"I rock a three piece. You better pick at least one hot bridesmaid." He takes my hand and leads me back to my chair. "Come on, now all we can do is wait."

Alex and Parker return and the waiting begins. It's the hardest four hours of my life. I'm inundated by memories of Mason. Standing outside my apartment insisting I go on a date with him, smiling down at me as I cuddled a baby panda bear, whispering filthy things in my ear as he fucks me. Pushing me outside my comfort zone, teaching me to trust, changing me. Loving me.

"Where's Cody?" I ask.

"With Macy and Devon at Mason's house. He's fine. Doesn't know," Parker replies.

"Are you okay?" I ask Parker, moving to sit beside him. I've been so focused on my own fear and pain, I haven't given a thought to his brothers.

"I wish Roberts hadn't killed the guy. So I could do it…slowly."

"While I watch and cheer you on," I agree. Our revenge plans are interrupted by the nurse.

"Reed family? Mason is settled in his room. You can see him now."

"Thank you," I cry, jumping to my feet.

She leads us to another smaller waiting room. "Only two at a time," she cautions. "He's heavily sedated."

As bad as I want to dart to him, I can't do that to his brothers. Squeezing each of their hands, I whisper, "Go."

After fifteen minutes that seem like an eternity, Alex returns, his eyes red and swollen. "Go on in, Ev. Parker's still in with him."

Nothing could have prepared me for the sight of my huge, strong, larger-than-life man looking so small and helpless. Dark circles ring his eyes and his skin is white as the sheets beneath him. Wires and tubes lead every which way and a heart monitor beeps monotonously.

I'm equally shocked by the sight of Parker sitting with his face buried in the edge of the bed, his shoulders shaking with sobs. I run my hand down his spine, and he turns, wrapping his arms around my back and pressing his face to my stomach. I don't know how long we stay that way, crying and holding each other.

I run my hand through Parker's hair, so like Mason's. His hair was just beginning to grow back out again. "Sorry, Ev," Parker says as he sits up, his voice hoarse.

"Don't be."

"He practically raised us. Aunt Linda and Uncle Logan took us in, but it was Mason we always went to when we had a problem."

"He relies on you too. I've seen it. I've never seen brothers as close as you three."

Parker reaches to squeeze Mason's hand. "You wake the fuck up, you bastard. You got people who love you, who depend on you. Cody needs you to teach him to be a man. And there's a beautiful woman here you need to make your wife. Wake up, buddy, or she's fair game."

"He told you?" I whisper.

"Yes."

"I didn't say yes. I should've said yes."

Parker chuckles and shakes his head. "When have you ever given into him the first time he's asked? I laughed my ass off watching him chase you." He takes my hand. "He knew you were going to marry him, Ev. Wasn't a doubt in his smug little mind."

"I am going to marry him. Because he's going to beat this. Can you give me a minute with him?"

"Of course, honey." He kisses my cheek. "I always wanted a sister," he adds before walking out.

The steady beep of the heart monitor drones on as I lay down beside Mason, careful not to disturb any tubes or wires. I rest my forehead against his head, closing my eyes at the tickle of his hair on my face. "Yes, Mason. Yes. I'll marry you. Do you hear me, sweetheart? You have to fight harder than you've ever fought in the ring. You're a champion. You can do this. I love you, and I'm waiting. I'm right beside you where I belong. I'm waiting."

Two days pass while I camp by Mason's bedside. Two excruciating days begging him to open his eyes, to squeeze my hand, to show me he's still here. Still beside me.

The doctors aren't sure why he won't wake and can't predict when—or if—he will. They're starting to talk about the possibility of brain damage from lack of oxygen. The waiting room is always full. His brothers, fighters and members of his gym, and women he's helped over the years flood in to show their support. I don't really see them since I don't leave his room. I have to be here when he wakes up. He has to wake up.

The gray sky fits the day perfectly. Ian pulls me closer to him, tucking me against his side as thunder rumbles in the distance. It mixes with the drone of the minister's words until I can't differentiate between them.

I don't want to be here. This isn't where I'm supposed to be. "It's okay to cry, Pup," Ian whispers as we watch the silver casket sink into the earth.

"I can't."

Alex and Parker take turns hugging me before leaving me to stare at the gravestone. "It's not his real name," I murmur. "He couldn't even be buried under his real name." For some reason, that pulls me under and I'm able to shed a few tears for the man I once worshipped. Don't all girls worship their daddies?

"You know who he is, and I'm sure that means more to him than anything. He got to see his daughter and hear her forgiveness before he died."

"Thanks to Mason," I sob. "Take me to him. That's where I belong."

Ian insists on stopping to eat on the way back to the hospital. "You're wasting away, Ev. Mason will never forgive me if you're skin and bones when he wakes."

When he wakes. We all keep saying that, though the chances grow slimmer each passing day. It's late afternoon when I return to the hospital. Mary, Mason's day nurse smiles at me when I enter and chirps, "Good strong heartbeat today." She always tries to say something positive and I'm so grateful for it. Before I can respond, a strange buzzing fills my ears and the floor rushes to meet me.

Shit. My jaw hurts. And some asshole is flashing a bright light in my face. "What happened?" I mumble, trying to get up.

"Sit up slowly, dear," Mary advises. "You fainted. Does your head hurt?"

Parker kneels on my other side, a worried look on his face. "Did you hit your head, Ev?"

"No, my jaw, but I'm all right." They help me into a chair like I'm an eighty year old lady.

"Are you dizzy?" Mary asks.

"No, just a bit nauseous. It comes and goes. It'll pass."

"Damn it, Everly." I look up in surprise at Parker's stern tone. "You can't do this. You need to eat and get some sleep."

"I slept nearly seven hours last night," I inform him, gesturing to the cot beside Mason's bed. "And Ian force fed me a roast beef sandwich not an hour ago."

"Probably stress," Mary says softly, turning to Parker. "But why don't you step out and I'll give Everly a quick exam?"

"Really, I'm fine," I insist.

"Do what she says," Parker growls, pulling the door shut behind him.

"Are you pregnant?" she asks.

"No."

"Are you sure?"

"Unless scar tissue can miraculously heal, yeah, I'm sure."

"I'm sorry. You're probably a little dehydrated. Why don't you let me take a small urine sample? Then I'll set your bodyguard's mind at ease." She nods toward the hall where Parker waits.

"Okay," I relent, eager to take the focus off of me and put it back on Mason where it belongs. Mary returns quickly with a little plastic cup, and I take it to the restroom. There's no way to hand someone a warm cup of your piss without it being awkward. After I give it to her, she excuses herself, and Parker comes back in.

"I wish you'd go home and rest," he says.

"I'm just a bit dehydrated. I'll grab a Gatorade and be fine."

"I'll get you one," he volunteers, dropping a kiss on my head on his way out. These Reed brothers really know how to take care of a girl. All three of them have such soft hearts under those hard muscles.

I'm lying in bed beside Mason, tracing his flower tattoos with my fingertip when Mary returns, a guarded look on her face. "We need to talk, Everly," she warns, and I sit up as she takes a seat.

"So, not dehydrated?" I guess. Shit. I really can't get sick right now.

"Everly, dear, you're pregnant."

My laugh is bitter at the sound of words I know can't be true. "That's impossible."

"What exactly did your doctor say about your condition?"

"That the formation of scar tissue would make the chances of conceiving astronomical." She doesn't need to know how I was scarred.

"But not impossible," she points out. "I ran the test three times. I don't know what it means for you, whether you can carry to term, but you are pregnant." Oh god. A baby. Mason's baby. I'd give anything for that to be true. "My husband is an O.B. in this hospital. Let me call him and I'm sure he'll see you."

Numb, I nod, and she smiles, making the call. "Half an hour, room 114."

I've been so focused on our conversation and the bombshell she's dropped on me, I failed to notice Parker standing in the doorway, his jaw on the floor. "You're pregnant?" he whispers, a smile spreading across his face. "I thought you were..."

"Barren? Me too. Don't get your hopes up. I won't believe it's possible until the O.B. confirms it." It's a wonder I don't have whiplash, the way he grabs my hand and pulls me from the room.

"Room 114," Mary calls after him.

Emotions and feelings have never been my friends. I've spent years developing a stunning lack of give a shit. It's how I cope. There have been times I wondered if a person can become a sociopath by choice. Just stop feeling. For years, my emotions were stunted, inhibited. All I wanted was stability and peace so I avoided anything that threatened my little bubble of safety. And I confess, I sometimes want to crawl right back to who I was.

But calm and predictable devolve into dull and mundane. By running from the pain, I also missed the joy. It's true I never cried, but I also rarely laughed or felt real happiness. Until Mason's persistent pursuit changed everything. He splashed color across my monochrome existence, let the sun burn through a somber sky to illuminate my path back to happiness. He made me feel again.

Emotions I've spent a lifetime repressing surge through me as I sit at Mason's bedside contemplating the life-altering news I've just received. I'm going to have a baby. The obstetrician assured me after an exam and ultrasound, that I should have no difficulty carrying to term. Apparently, the only obstacle was conceiving, and Mason's super sperm burrowed right through that.

Joyful tears mingle with tears of sorrow and despair. I'm going to have Mason's child. My mind conjures a mini Mason with bright blue eyes and a crooked grin while my hand travels to palm my belly. There's a part of him growing in there, part of both of us, and I couldn't be more thrilled. But he doesn't know. He may never know.

"Stop it," Parker scolds, handing me a tissue. He stayed with me during the O.B. visit, even when they ran a probe up my vagina for the ultrasound. I made him stand by my head where he couldn't see anything, but still, it was awkward having his hand in mine while the doctor rooted around like he was searching for treasure.

"What?"

"Whatever you're obsessing about. Think about how fucking thrilled Mason will be when you tell him."

"And if he doesn't wake up?" I finally put a voice to my worst fear.

A wave of pain flows over his face before he forces a smile. "You'll still be stuck with us, Ev, so get used to it. You're family. I'm going to be amoeba's favorite uncle."

"Amoeba?"

"That's what it looked like to me."

"It's not an amoeba." I giggle.

"Okay, how about parasite? I mean, technically it is."

"Now you're asking for a foot in your ass."

Alex rushes into the room, his blond curls bouncing, and stares at me in shock. "Is it true? You're pregnant?"

How the hell? "Parker!"

He holds his palms up. "I texted him. No one else knows."

"Oh, Everly. This is the best news." Alex hugs me like he may never get another chance. "You have to take care of yourself. Eat, rest. You can't keep staying here."

"I won't miss a meal, but I'm sleeping here," I insist.

"You should at least go home at night. We won't leave him alone."

"Not going to happen. My ass is right here until he wakes up."

Before Alex can respond, a hoarse voice replies, "Give up, Alex. She's stubborn as hell. You'll never win." My tears before are nothing compared to the deluge I let loose on Mason's shoulder. I don't even remember crawling in his bed.

Parker fetches him some water, and Alex goes for a nurse while I completely lose it. "Shh, stop, Panda. I'm okay. I'm good."

"I was so afraid I'd never talk to you again. I talked your ear off when you were unconscious."

"You said yes," he says, cupping my cheek.

"You heard me?"

"Yep, and I'm holding you to it. A near death yes is still a yes."

"I don't know. I read the loss of a spleen can dull your sexual performance."

"I'll disavow you of that notion soon enough."

His cocky smile makes me laugh. "I missed you."

"I knew you were here. I just couldn't make myself wake up. But I knew you were beside me."

"Always."

Mason spends a few more days in the hospital before he's released with orders to rest for a few weeks. I still haven't told him about the baby. The man's heart stopped twice and I don't want to be responsible for a third time. I need to tell him soon, though, or his brothers are going to give it away with their excitement.

He's such a damn grouch after being cooped up at home the last week, and it doesn't help that he's been warned off all sexual activity for another. Nearly three weeks without sex is an eternity to him. To me, too, if I'm being honest.

Tonight's the night. I'm going to tell him. My hands shake all day at the thought. I told him I couldn't get pregnant. What if he thinks I tricked him, trapped him into having a kid with me? He's already gained one kid unexpectedly. What if he doesn't want another? I'm sure my psycho pregnancy hormones aren't helping my judgement toward the situation.

Parker shows up to pick up Cody for a sleepover, and grins at me. I nod at him, assuring him I plan to tell Mason today, and get a wink in response.

Mason scowls. "Quit flirting with my girl before I kick your ass."

"Take it easy, old man. Don't want to give yourself heart palpitations. I'm going."

As soon as they're out the door, I turn to Mason, my stomach churning. "I need to tell you something."

His look is guarded as he sits across from me. My hands twist in my lap, and he reaches to still them. "What's wrong?"

There's really no way to sugarcoat it so I just blurt out, "I'm pregnant."

His mouth falls open. "Pregnant?" he whispers as if tasting the word. Confusion clouds his face. "But I thought you couldn't?"

"So did I," I reply with a heavy sigh. My chest aches with the deep desire for his reaction to be positive. "Chances I would conceive were infinitesimal. I know you trusted me when I told you we didn't need condoms. I swear I thought we were safe."

Leaning forward, he puts his hands on my knees. "Evie, is this going to put your health at risk?"

"No, the doctor assures me my pregnancy should progress normally." My anxiety increases the longer he fails to react one way or the other.

"We're having a baby," he says.

"Yes."

I'm stunned when he falls to his knees, wraps his arms around my waist and presses his face to my belly. My hands thread through his soft hair as he's overcome by the news. His eyes are glassy and red rimmed when he looks up at me and murmurs, "Thank you."

"You had a little something to do with it," I reply, swallowing the lump in my throat.

"Fuck, yeah I did!" The couch shakes as he bounds to his feet and shouts, "How badass are my swimmers!" A giant smile is plastered on his face and he paces the room like a caged panther. "Wait until I tell Alex and Parker! Evie!" I'm swept into his arms and spun around the room. "We're having a baby!"

Relieved laughter pours from my lips. "I'm so glad you're happy."

"Happy? Sweetheart, I'm fucking ecstatic. I don't know what to do with myself."

"Your brothers know already," I tell him.

He stops pacing and stares at me. "You told them first?"

"I found out when you were in the hospital. A few hours before you woke up, actually. Parker went to the doctor with me, then he told Alex. I told him to keep his big mouth shut."

"You've known for a week? Why didn't you tell me?"

"You were sick. I didn't want to give you a heart attack."

He pulls me into his arms again. "I should take you over my knee."

"Hmm." I burrow my face into his neck, inhaling the scent of his skin. "That would probably lead to activities you aren't cleared to participate in."

"Are you happy, Panda? Is this what you want?"

I gaze into eyes the color of a summer sky. "More than I've ever wanted anything."

"I love you."

"Enough to marry me before the baby's born?"

"Let's go to Vegas tonight."

Laughing, I kiss his jaw. "Vegas sounds good, but we have to wait until everyone can go. Alex and Parker would never forgive you if we eloped, and Ian would kick my ass."

Mason caresses my belly and murmurs, "A little Evie."

"A little Mason," I retort.

"Or one of each. Twins do run in the family, you know," he teases with a smirk.

Damn. Hadn't thought of that.

Chapter Fourteen

Mason

"I want to take you ring shopping today," I inform Evie, sinking my fingers into the soft curve of her waist. Her hesitation sends a streak of fear down my spine. Is she backing out?

"I wanted to talk to you about that. I'm not big on jewelry and I have an idea." She peeks up at me. "What would you think about tattooing our rings instead?"

Christ, this woman is perfect for me. "It's permanent," I remind her.

"So are we."

"I fucking love you, Evie." Her lips part in surprise, and I slip my tongue between them. If Cody wasn't in the next room, I'd throw her down and taste every inch of this woman. She drives me out of my mind.

Her hands run through my hair, settling on the nape of my neck. "So, you like the idea?"

"I love it. It'll hurt, though, love. Hands are a painful choice for a first tattoo." Ridiculous, though I'm covered in ink, I can't bear the thought of her under the needle. Of her hurting in any way.

"It won't be my first. I want another on my hip at the same time." A smile softens her face. "You told me a tattoo should mean something to you. Something you'll want for the rest of your life.

I know what that is now." She lays two fingers on the dip between her hip and pelvis. "And where I want it."

"Tell me."

She giggles when I lift her up and sit her on the kitchen counter. "Nope. Not until it's done. Macy is a great artist. She drew it for me. I'm just not sure where to go."

"You'll go to my guy."

"I will, huh?" she teases, and I step between her legs.

"Yes, and since you'll be practically naked in his chair, I'm going with you." Her lips brush my neck as I trail my hands up her inner thighs.

"Neanderthal," she says fondly. "When can we go?"

"I'll see if Tony can get us in after hours tonight if you're sure."

"I'm sure."

For someone who isn't nervous about getting inked, Evie sure is fidgety on the drive to Tony's shop. I rest my hand on her knee for a second before we get out of the car. "It's not as painful as you think. Anytime you need a break, just say so."

"I can do this," she says with a hesitant grin.

"I know, baby."

A bell on the door dings when we enter and Tony comes out to lock it behind us. Tony is a six foot four mass of tattoos and piercings, and Evie's eyes widen when she shakes his hand. "Welcome, honey. I hear this is your first ink. Are you nervous?"

"A little," she confesses, smiling at him.

"Reed looks more anxious than you. The big guys are always like that. Covered in tats and can't stand to see their girl get a needle. Do you have a sketch for me?"

Evie nods and waves me away. They spend a few minutes discussing the drawing and changing a few things. When they're both happy with it, Tony disappears into the back room to prepare the stencil.

"You can't go back with me," Evie insists. "I don't want you to see it until it's finished."

"Evie, you're going to be in his chair with your pants down. I'm coming. I won't look. I'll just hold your hand."

"I can do this by myself." God, I want to spank the stubbornness out of her sometimes.

"You can, but you aren't."

"Fine," she huffs. "What are you getting other than the ring?"

"Oh no, I'll show you mine when you show me yours."

"Fair enough." She laughs. I follow Evie and Tony back to the private room and watch her climb nervously into the chair.

"Pull your shorts down over your hips," Tony instructs, and she glances at me as she complies. Whatever she's getting is going to be sexy as hell, but I don't like Tony seeing so much of her.

I promised I wouldn't look, so I scoot a stool to the head of the chair, facing her. I won't peek if she really doesn't want me to. "Panties have to come down a few inches," Tony says, and Evie's face glows as she lowers them to just above her hairline. Evie watches Tony open the needles and prepare his gun. "Are you ready, honey?"

Evie nods. I take her hand and she damn near breaks mine when Tony starts the outline. "Relax," Tony advises. "It's a tender area for your first tattoo, but you're doing great. Let me know if you need a break." Gradually, her hand loosens and she only squeezes when he gets close to her hip bone.

"Does it hurt worse than you expected?" I ask, tucking her hair behind her ear.

"It's kind of numb now. Really stung in the beginning, though."

"Finger is going to be worse, honey." Tony peeks up at her. "Just so you know." The gun ceases and I know Tony's wiping away the excess ink by the grimace on Evie's face. "All done. Come have a look." Tony leads her to the three way mirror.

"It's perfect," she breathes. I'm allowed to turn around once the tattoo has been bandaged.

"Let's do the rings next. Mason's art is going to take a few hours. Who's first?"

"Let me," Everly says. "Before I lose my nerve."

"Rest your hand here."

"Fuck," Evie hisses as the needle starts to move. The cords in her neck stand out and she grits her teeth against the pain.

"You're doing so good, baby," I assure her, stroking her other hand.

"Will it take long?" she asks, her voice timorous.

"Just a few minutes, honey," Tony replies. "Hang in there."

Evie sighs with relief, her eyes glassy with unshed tears when he finishes. Tony wraps the tattoo in a thin layer of gauze and places a band aid around it. "You've got a tough one here, Reed. Didn't even cry. The girls usually do. I've had a few guys change their mind on a toe or finger tat once I get started."

"That's my girl," I murmur, kissing her neck. "How does your hip feel?"

"Like it's on fire."

"Are you sorry you did it?"

"No, I didn't expect it to tickle."

"Smartass." She jumps when I smack her ass before taking my turn in the chair. Evie stays beside me while I get a black band tattooed around my ring finger to match hers—it does hurt like a bitch—but I insist she leave when Tony prepares the stencil for my ribs.

"The T.V. remote is on the desk," Tony tells her as she heads to the lounge. "Make yourself at home."

"Mason Reed getting hitched. Never thought I'd see the day," Tony says when she's out of earshot. We've known each other for years so I knew he'd have something to say.

"Fuck, man. Neither did I." I laugh, stripping off my shirt.

"You sure about getting her name, man? You know my opinion on that."

"Evie's it for me. I'll be back for another name soon."

Tony laughs, lining up the transfer paper on my skin. "You knocked her up, didn't you, you bastard?"

"I can't help it if my swimmers are superhuman."

"Congratulations, man," he says sincerely. "I'm happy for you. Now hold still."

Two and a half hours later we're all bandaged up and heading home.

"How does he lose one shoe?" I ask, leaning to look under the couch, and Evie giggles.

"He's a boy."

"Found it!" Cody cries, running in from the back patio, waving his sneaker. "I forgot I used it to prop up my Hot Wheel ramp."

"Good job," Evie tells him, watching him painstakingly tie his laces. I taught him a few days ago and he's just getting the hang of it.

"Why do we have to move? I like it here."

"You'll love our new house. You'll have your own room and I think your daddy has a little surprise for you."

His eyes light up. "What is it?"

"You'll have to wait and see," Evie teases.

I have a little surprise for her as well. We've discussed what changes we want to make with the remodel, but she has no idea I hired the contractors weeks ago and they've just finished. The furniture we picked out was delivered just yesterday.

No sooner than the engine is off, Cody is out the door and bouncing toward the house. "Look at him. You got him all worked up." I wrap my arm around Evie's waist, careful of her new tattoo.

"Hey, you put in a porch swing! I love it." Evie grins and curls up on the wooden swing. I know the wraparound porch on this place, and the den, are what sold her on the house.

"I may have made a few more improvements since you were here last." Weeks recovering from gunshot wounds gave me plenty of time to arrange the remodel. I'm sure the contractors thought I was a pain in the ass for rushing the work, but I paid them well.

The shock and joy on Evie's face when she steps into the living room is worth every cent I spent to surprise her. "When did you do this?"

"Do you like it? We can change whatever you want. It's

ready for us to move in when we get back from Vegas."

"You sneaky son of a bitch," she exclaims, throwing her arms around my neck. "You did all this behind my back."

"Hey, I have to get you moved in before you change your mind."

"Never going to happen. You're stuck with me," she replies, slipping her tongue between my lips and giving me a long hot kiss.

"Quit it before you make me hard," I growl.

"Daddy! Evie! Look! The Hulk!" Cody cries.

"Looks like he found his room." I chose one of the downstairs bedrooms for him, a good distance from mine and Evie's. I'd hate for him to overhear the dirty things I plan to do her. The bedroom adjacent to his will be for the live-in nanny I plan to hire. With our work for Striking Back, we need to be able to leave at a moment's notice, and I don't want to drag him out of bed to leave him with a babysitter.

"Is this my room? Can it be? Please?" Cody rushes into us at the bedroom door.

"Well." I pretend to think about it. "I really like those bunk beds, but since Evie will just steal the top bunk, I think you'd better take this room."

"Yay!" He grabs Evie's hand and tugs her toward the 3-D mural painted on the far wall. I hired a local artist, and he did an amazing job. The Hulk appears to be smashing through the wall and coming right at us.

Cody digs into the toy box in the corner while I lead Evie to her favorite room. I left the brown carpet that she loved and had the walls painted a deep red. That isn't what causes the catch in her breathing or her soft exclamation, "Oh, Mason."

All three shelves are now full of books. She runs her fingers across the spines, reading the titles, and for a second I think she might cry. "How did you know what books to get? These are my favorites."

"I may have peeked at your Goodreads account when you left it signed in. These are from your list marked Favorites." I gesture to the wall beside us before pointing to the next. "Those are from a list titled To Be Read. The others were listed as Recommended Reads."

I'm nearly knocked off my feet as she barrels into my chest. "You are too damn good to me."

Cradling her head against my shoulder, I run my fingers through her soft hair. "I know it won't always be easy to live on the grounds of a domestic violence shelter. There will be lots of women and kids running around. My brothers and their drama. I want you to have a place to escape and relax."

"I love you," she murmurs.

"I love you too."

"I was talking to the room." She grins up at me, and I smack her ass.

"I'm going to fuck you in front of that fireplace the first cold night we have."

"Come on, winter."

Cody charges into the room. "Wow, look at all the books!"

I scoop him up. "This is Evie's library."

"Cool. There are guys digging out back. I saw a dump truck."

"Uh-huh. Let's go have a look."

Cody wanders around while I point out the progress of the construction to Evie. A few walls of the apartment house are up and the framers are hard at work. Between the apartments and our back door is a large frame with a few glass panels installed.

"A greenhouse?" Evie asks.

"Not exactly. I'm having a large sunroom built, large enough to house an in ground pool. We'll be able to swim no matter the weather."

"Cody will love that." She turns to study me. "You've thought of everyone but you. Where's your escape?"

"Ah, you haven't seen the basement yet. Pool table, bar, every video game known to man."

"You have a man cave? No girls allowed?" Her little smirk is so sexy.

"I'll need someone to bring me beer and show me her titties."

"I'll start looking at applicants."

"Spitfire," I growl, pulling her against me.

Cody returns, a grin on his flushed face. "Was The Hulk room my surprise, Daddy?"

"One of them." He giggles as I sweep him onto my shoulders. "Let's go see what's in the garage."

His eyes widen at the sight of the little red bicycle. "I don't know how to ride a bike," he worries.

"It has training wheels so you won't fall," I assure him, settling him on the seat. A few minutes later, he's riding around the driveway, smiling from ear to ear.

Evie lays her head on my shoulder, and I tuck her little body against mine, cupping my hand over her belly. "We're going to be so happy here," she says with a sigh.

It's exactly what I wanted to hear.

We're all packed for our weekend in Vegas. We booked rooms for Alex, Parker, Ian, Macy, and Amy as well so we can share the occasion with our friends and family. Twenty-four hours from now Evie will be my wife.

Cody is asleep when we retreat to our bedroom.

"We need a proposal story I can actually tell people," Evie complains, grinning at me. "It's bad enough the story of how we met includes us being naked."

"Tell them the truth."

"I'm not saying you proposed with your face in my crotch."

"Like you said, baby. We met naked. I think it fits us perfectly." I pull my shirt over my head while she rolls her eyes at me. "We can take the bandages off our tats," I remind her as she strips off her tank top and shorts.

"You first," she replies with a smirk.

"No way, baby. I can't wait any longer to see what means enough to you to permanently mark your beautiful skin."

I'm rewarded with a soft smile. "Okay." She bites her lip when I kneel and slowly remove the gauze. It's not the sight of the bright yellow daisy that stuns me, but the script beneath it that spells my name. My name permanently etched on her soft skin.

"In Norse mythology, daisies represent love and fertility. Sensuality and motherhood." Her eyes tear and her hand tightens in my hair. "You've given me all those things."

I rest my forehead against her bare belly, trying to get a grip on my roiling emotions. I've chased this woman until I was half crazy and even when I caught her, I could never be sure she loved me like I do her. But she does. She does.

"Do you like it?" she asks softly.

"Sweetheart, there are no words."

She tilts my head up to look at her. "You don't mind I copied your flower idea?"

"I'm honored." I lead her to the bed and pull her into my lap. "It was my mother that taught me to appreciate the beauty of flowers. She spent hours in her garden, explaining to me what each represented and why she loved them. They're my happiest memories of her, listening to her in the garden. It brought me peace, made me happy. I haven't felt that since she died. Until I met you. Looking at you, being with you, brings me the same peace and joy."

Tears pour down her face. "I'm not good at this, Mason, at explaining how I feel about you. You say the sweetest things and I just can't...this is the best way I know to show you how much I love you. How I need you. You're so important to me. Like you said, there just aren't words."

"It's perfect, love. And you show me how you feel every day."

Evie stands and looks into my eyes while her fingers graze the edge of my bandage, seeking permission. I nod, and she peels it away. Her lip trembles and she shakes her head. "You...did Tony tell you I got your name?"

"No. I had this planned before you decided on a tattoo. Tony drew it up weeks ago."

Her fingertips trace the life-like Panda resting on my

ribcage. It's no cartoon rendering. The detail is amazing, and Evie's name is nestled among the pile of bamboo surrounding the bear. "I love it."

"Do you?"

Closing her eyes, she presses a feather light kiss on the ink. "It's beautiful. It's me. I'm your Panda."

"Rare and special," I murmur, repeating my words from our first real date when I took her to the zoo.

We remove the band aids circling our fingers and lay back on the bed, holding our hands up to admire our rings. "Tomorrow, some minister or Elvis impersonator is going to make it official, but this is all I need. You're mine, Evie."

"I'm yours."

Epilogue

Evie

One Year Later

We burst from the courtroom in a crowd of smiles and laughter. Alex, Parker, and Ian all hug Cody, who has just officially become my son. Even with Mason's connections and Jamie's fifteen year prison sentence it took forever to get her parental rights terminated.

Cody has grown into a happy outgoing boy who does well in school. It was just after our wedding that Cody asked if he could call me Mom, and I approached Mason with the idea of adopting him. Needless to say, he was on board.

Some mornings I sit up in bed and gaze at my sleeping husband, then at our baby boy in his bassinet and wonder if I'm still asleep and dreaming. A little over a year ago, I was alone and content to stay that way. Now, I'm surrounded by the one thing I've always craved. Family.

I'm his.

The End.

Acknowledgments

Thank you for reading! If you enjoyed this story, I hope you'll consider leaving a review on Amazon. It doesn't need to be long, a few sentences that share your opinion of the book would be very much appreciated.

I love to connect with readers! Please stalk me at the following links.
https://facebook.com/authorsmshade
https://facebook.com/smshadebooks
https://twitter.com/authorSMShade
http://www.smshade.blogspot.com

Would you like to be a part of the S.M. Shade Fan Club? As a member of the S.M. Shade Book Group, you'll be entered in giveaways for gift cards, e-books, and Advanced Read Copies. Be a part of the private Facebook group and privy to excerpts and cover art of upcoming books before the public. You can request to join at:
https://facebook.com/groups/694215440670693

Thanks to Jolanda Lovestoread for tweeting my books endlessly. She has wonderful book suggestions. Follow her here.
https://twitter.com/JolandaNovella

Special Thanks go to Lissa Jay, Joanna Hughes, and Jamie Lauritano for beta reading and saving me from embarrassing plot holes and ridiculous mistakes.

Last, but not least, thanks to all the book bloggers and page owners who make it possible for Indie authors to get their stories out there. We couldn't do it without you.

More from S.M.

Coming Soon:
Parker, Striking Back : Book Three (10/2015)
Alex, Striking Back : Book Four (01/2016)

Everly, Striking Back: Book One

The first time I met Mason Reed, we were standing naked in a bank, surrounded by guns.

That should have been a warning.

An MMA champion, trainer, and philanthropist, but not a man who gives up easily, Mason is trouble dipped in ink and covered in muscle.

Growing up in foster care, I'm well aware that relationships are temporary, and I do my best to avoid them. After a sheet clenching one night stand, I'm happy to move on, but Mason pursues me relentlessly. Sweet, caring, protective, and at times, a bossy control freak, this persistent man has climbed inside my heart, and I can't seem to shake him.

After saving me from a life threatening situation, he's also won something much harder to obtain. My trust. But does he deserve it? Is his true face the one he shows the world? Or is his charitable, loving manner only a thin veneer?

This book contains sexual situations and is intended for ages 18 and older.

The Last Woman, All That Remains : Book One

When Abby Bailey meets former model and actor, Airen Holder, in a darkened department store, romance is the last thing on her mind. A plague has decimated the population, leaving Abby to raise her son alone in a world without electricity, clean water, or medical care. Her only priority is survival.

Traumatized by the horror of the past months, Abby and Airen become a source of comfort for one another. Damaged by her past and convinced Airen is out of her league, Abby is determined to keep their relationship platonic. However, Airen is a hard man to resist, especially after he risks his life to save hers.

When a man named Joseph falls unconscious in their yard, and Abby nurses him back to health, everything changes. How does love differ in this new post apocalyptic world? Can three unlikely survivors live long enough to find their place in it?

This is the first of the All that Remains series and can also be read as a stand alone novel. It contains violence and sexual situations and is recommended for ages 18 and older.

Falling Together, All That Remains : Book Two

In the aftermath of a global nightmare, Abby Holder is living her dream. Married to the love of her life, Airen, and surrounded by friends and family, it seems she's found her happily ever after.

But the struggle of living in a post-plague world is never ending. When circumstances take Airen far away, she's faced with the devastating realization he may be lost to her forever. Broken-hearted, she turns to Joseph, her best friend and the only one who understands her pain. After all, he loves Airen too.

The sound of a car horn in the middle of the night changes everything, leaving Abby caught between the two most important men in her life. After surviving the worst the world could throw at them, Airen, Abby, and Joseph must face the most brutal human experience...true love. Can they overcome the betrayal, the hurt feelings, and jealousy to do what's right for the ones they love?

Their circumstances are far from ordinary. Perhaps the answer is extraordinary as well.

This book includes sexual scenes between two men and is intended for ages 18 and older.

InfiniteTies, All That Remains : Book Three

The more you look to the future, the more the past pursues you.
Abby, Airen, and Joseph have fought and suffered to come together. All they want is to move forward and raise their family with the love they never had.
Unfortunately, the re-appearance of former friends and enemies complicates their lives, threatening to expose closely guarded secrets. With a vital rescue looming, their relationship isn't the only thing at risk. Can they let go of the past in order to hang on to a future with each other?

This is the conclusion of the All That Remains Trilogy.
Warning : Contains sex scenes between a woman and two men, violence, and references to child abuse. Recommended for ages 18 and older.

Printed in Great Britain
by Amazon